FOREVER
london

FOREVER 18 BOOK 2

USA Today Bestselling Author
Heather Young-Nichols

Forever London
Forever 18 Book 2
USA Today Bestselling Author
Heather Young-Nichols

heatheryoungnichols.com

ALSO BY HEATHER YOUNG-NICHOLS

New Adult Romance

Forever 18

Forever Grayson

Heavy Hitter

Pushing Daisies

Daisy

Van

Bonham

Daltrey

Mack

Courting Chaos

Cross

Holiday Bites

All I Want

All of Me

The Fallout Series

Last Good Thing

A Little More Touch Me

Hard to Say Yes

Paranormal Romance

The Empowered Series

The Gremlin Prince

The Goblin War

Dark Coven

Witch of Warwick

Doomed by Magic

1

LONDON

There was one thing I knew for sure, and it was that I wasn't ever getting caught up with feelings like Grayson Cook. A lot of people say that, but I was determined. I'd fuck women, even regularly, but I wasn't doing the relationship thing.

I'd done that in high school and that led to a heartbreak that I never wanted to experience in the future. I couldn't imagine caring about someone so much again, then *poof*. They were gone.

Not ever going to happen again.

"Of all of us, though, I knew it'd be Grayson," Jamison said right before taking a nice, long drink of his beer. His dirty blond hair hung in a mess.

The seven of us were on our tour bus, a couple of

weeks into the tour. And there were *seven* of us. The band: me, lead guitar; Grayson Cook, our lead singer; Lennox Weaver, rhythm guitar; Thatcher Hoffman, bass; and Jamison McCall, drums. On top of that, we'd been joined by Lilah Chambers, Grayson's girl, and her best friend Becca. The two of them were also our stylists for the tour.

It was a cozy fit, but when we weren't being grouches, there was plenty of room and the women were trying really hard to not get in the way.

"Why's that?" Grayson asked. He sat over on the couch with a beer in his hand and his woman in his lap. His dark hair looked like Lilah had been running her fingers through it. Which she was doing lightly right now.

Lilah had her feet shoved between Grayson's legs like she was trying to warm them up. We'd just finished a show and were on the road to the next one. We did keep the bus fairly cool, and she was in a pair of cotton shorts and a tank top—her pajamas, I assumed. She had her chocolate hair pulled into two small braids on each side of her head, and her hazel eyes danced as she watched Grayson. It was a little nauseating, to be honest.

"I don't know," Jamison continued. "It just seems like you."

"Really?" Lennox cocked his head to the side. "I figured we'd all hold out and live the rock-star life until we were old."

"Rock-star life?" Becca asked, as if she didn't know what he was referring to. "What exactly is that?" Becca was the opposite of her best friend. Lilah had the shorter dark hair while Becca's was long, blonde, and curly. They were about the same size, though.

With the smile playing at the corners of her mouth, it was clear she knew exactly what she was doing. Stirring up trouble, or trying to see if she could make Grayson uncomfortable. I didn't give a shit. I'd tell her exactly what we'd done on the road so far, but for Grayson's sake, I wouldn't.

He and Lilah as a couple were new and I wasn't hitting *that* bees' nest with a stick.

"Quit making trouble," Lilah told her best friend.

"Me?" She held her hand against her chest as if outraged. "I would never."

Lilah smiled and shook her head. I supposed if Grayson had to hook up permanently with someone, I was glad it was a woman like Lilah. She didn't come off as bothered by anything he'd done in his past and she was chill in general. He could've done a lot worse.

The only downside was that with the women being here, the dynamic had shifted. There was no denying that. So far, we hadn't wanted to do any after-parties, but I was curious to see how it would go when we did.

Most of the time, I was up later into the night playing with my guitar. Or one of the other guys and I worked on new material. That was the great thing about how we worked together. Whenever the mood hit, whoever wanted to work on a new song or something, we did it. There were no egos here where that was concerned.

After a while, almost everyone found their way to their bunks, leaving just Thatch and me. Grayson had been my best friend since before we'd started the band, but all five of us were as tight as we could've been. We didn't have any issues like Courting Chaos had a while back with one of their members. Not a single one of us would even think about having sex with underage girls. Good thing they got rid of that guy.

That was fucked up.

"Do you regret this?" Thatcher asked as he popped another top off a beer.

"Regret what?" I strummed softly on the acoustic guitar that I used on the bus.

"This." He waved his hand around as if he meant *everything*, but I knew exactly what he was talking about.

"Nah. It wouldn't be better if Grayson was on the other bus."

"True, but it's only been a little while."

"I know. If he'd picked someone else, someone very un-Lilah like, then we'd probably have some problems. I think this is going to be fine."

"And when one of us wants to bring a woman back to the bus?"

"Lilah and Becca will have to learn to live with it," I said. He nodded as I changed keys. "If you think about it, this bus has enough room that we could add a few more people if we had to."

Our bus had been somewhat customized by the previous owners. There were eight bunks (four on each side) in bunk alley and a small lounge near the bag where we could've technically fit a couple of people who were cool with grabbing a sleeping bag on the floor. The bunks could fit two people, though you'd better like the person because it was going to be tight. Then we had the main living area with a couch, a nice table area, and a small kitchen. Oh, and the restroom was off to the side before bunk alley.

"Where the fuck would we put more people?" Thatcher scoffed.

"Eight bunks. Two people per bunk. Then sleeping bags on the floor in the back."

"I'm not sharing my fuckin' bunk."

My chuckle bounced my guitar on my leg. "No one's asking you to. I'm just saying."

Thatcher was quiet for a minute before he said, "I really hope there's no emergency."

There was no doubt the dynamic was changing. Or had already changed. That was bound to happen and we were going to have to roll with it.

I was happy for Grayson. If Lilah was what he wanted, then I wanted him to have her.

But it was easy for him. He didn't know the heartbreak that loving someone like that could bring. He'd seen it secondhand with me, but he didn't *know*. He hadn't *experienced* it and I hoped he never did.

As for me, there was no room in my heart or my life for love or anything close to it.

2

CHARLOTTE

"Unfortunately, your grades have slipped enough that we have to consider academic probation." The man sitting across from me was my advisor and when I'd gotten an email asking me to come in for an appointment, I hadn't known what I thought it would be about, but it hadn't been this.

Though I should've known.

My grades this semester haven't been the best. My focus had shit the bed and it was obviously showing.

Mr. Warner's blond hair was thinning, which aged him, but other than that, he was a good-looking man, sitting there with his dress shirt's top button undone and the sleeves rolled up to the elbows, something I've always thought was sexy, though not on him.

I might have had daddy issues, but it didn't lead to me trying to replace the love I didn't get from him with sexual proclivities that would earn me approval.

"What can I do?" I asked him, hoping it didn't come out sounding like I was offering something. I might not have had sex in a while, but I wasn't desperate and the ring on this man's finger said he was married. And even if that didn't stop me, the fact that his wife just had a baby would have.

"Study. Ask your professors for extra credit, though you know they rarely give it." He leaned forward and folded his hands under his chin. "And focus, Charlotte. I think your biggest issue is focus."

Don't I know it.

This semester had been rough, as far as my focus was concerned and I didn't know if it was senioritis at the end of my junior year or if I was just anxious for summer.

Or maybe this just wasn't the life that I wanted to lead. The one laid out by my father, where stepping out of line could ruin the entire family.

I wanted freedom. Excitement. To do something no one would ever expect of me. Not this safe "major in Political Science so that I could follow in Daddy's footsteps" planned bullshit.

Most of the time, I could reason that my father was doing what he did out of love. I wasn't abused. They didn't hit me or starve me and so many people had it so much worse. But I wouldn't wish this pressure on my worst enemy.

The pressure to measure up meant that I couldn't just be me.

"I don't suppose my father could buy my way out of this with a huge donation."

Mr. Warner snorted. He'd been advising me for three years, so he knew me enough to know that I was joking.

Joke was on him because I was half-joking. If I thought my family's money could help me, I might've used it. Maybe. Maybe not. But there had to be *some* benefit to being in the Andersen family.

"Sorry, Charlotte," Mr. Warner told me. "You know better." He watched as I nodded slowly and looked down at my fingers nervously battling each other. "This isn't high school. We won't be sending any letters home, no matter who your parents are. This is on you. As an adult. I can help you set up some study groups for your last couple of exams, but I expect that it's a little too late."

Yeah. It was. We were in exam week now and the semester was almost over.

"The good news is, you aren't failing anything, but you are on the verge of it. Do decently on your last two exams tomorrow and you'll come out of this, but the university doesn't like to lose any of our brightest students. Which you are. You've told me about the pressure your father puts on you and I can only imagine, but you have to decide if this is what *you* want. Is it?"

"A college education? Yes."

"Then you need to keep your head down and do the work."

I sighed. "I know. I have for almost three years."

He nodded. "I know. You're a fantastic student and told me once that you wanted an education so that once you have it, you can get away from that pressure. Has that changed?"

He remembered everything. "No."

"OK. Then let's turn this around. Do your best tomorrow and we can meet before you leave campus next week to make sure your plan for next year is solid. Maybe you're taking too many credits. We'll take a look at that."

"Thanks, Mr. Warner."

He gave me a nod of dismissal, which I took and left his office.

How humiliating was it that I'd been called to the university's equivalent to the principal's office for my bad grades. At least my parents wouldn't ever know that I'd stumbled. If they did, I'd never live it down.

It was hard having a perfect brother who did what was expected of him. I loved my brother, but man, he made it hard to be myself. Though he insisted that becoming a doctor was what he'd wanted to do since he'd been a kid, I always wondered if that idea had been planted there by the parents.

When I got back to my apartment, the one I shared with my best friend, Kenzie, I dropped my bag inside the door and kept walking until I was in my own room, where I could fling myself down, face first, onto my bed.

"Good meeting?" Kenzie asked from the area near my closet.

I pushed up so that I could see her. "The best. What are you doing?"

"Looking for a dress to wear to the party tonight." She turned back to my closet. "You have the best clothes."

My clothing was one of the only things that I had any say in. Of course, every decision still had to follow "the guidelines of propriety," as my mother called them. But with their money and my taste, I did have a pretty fantastic closet.

"What did Warner want?" She turned and put her fist on her hip, her long, auburn hair falling over her shoulders. "Are they giving you a super-smart student award?"

I snorted. "The opposite actually." She raised an eyebrow but waited for me to continue. "He wanted to talk to me about academic probation."

"What?" Her eyes widened.

"Yeah. I was surprised, too." That was a lie. "Wait. No, I wasn't." I took a deep breath and fell onto my back to stare up at the ceiling. "I've been struggling this semester."

The bed dipped beside me, so I knew that Kenzie had laid down too. "Why didn't you say something? I would've helped." I'd known that already. "Only you're way smarter than I am, so it probably wouldn't have helped."

The two of us giggled. "You're very smart."

"I do OK, but you're like *smart*, smart. Like so smart, I was surprised when you told me in high school you were going to major in Poli Sci in college.

I assumed you were off to med school like your brother and would be some famous surgeon or something."

My stomach tightened. "I don't like blood." Some would call that a trauma from the past, but I just didn't like the sight of blood and would never admit that anything in my history had influenced that.

"I know," she said quietly. "So what's going on?"

That was a question I didn't think I could fully answer just yet. "I don't know. This semester has just been... ugh. I don't know." I threw my arm over my face and groaned.

"It's one semester, Charlotte. Just one. You're not failing... are you?" she asked. I shook my head, moving my arm with it. "There you go. And it's not like they send report cards home because I know you're worried about your parents finding out."

"Yeah. Mr. Warner said the same thing. They'll only know if I tell them, but I have my last two exams tomorrow and there's nothing more beyond that I can do."

"Exactly. You'll have to let it go." She pushed off the bed and went back over to the closet. "Why did he wait so long to talk to you?"

"Because the first half of the semester was fine." I sat up to watch her paw through my clothes.

Kenzie and I were the same size with mostly the same proportions. Her breasts were slightly smaller, but not enough to make a difference in the fit. Otherwise, we had the same curves and she was around five-foot-four, which was only an inch over me. We got lucky having a best friend the same size.

"Then his wife had the baby, so he was out for a couple of weeks. This was really the first chance we've had."

"What shitty timing, having a baby."

We both giggled. Mr. Warner wasn't the problem. I was.

She held up this red, glittery dress that I'd only worn once, but I shook my head. That was too much for the party she was going to. I wouldn't be going with her because I now needed to review everything about my life. Or at least the material for the tests tomorrow.

Kenzie put it back then turned to me. "So why did this semester go off the rails? You're always so on top of things."

"I don't know," I told her, but that wasn't exactly true. "No. I know." I sighed. "I hate it."

"School?"

"Yes, but it's not school's fault," I said. She held up another blue dress that was summery and fun and that one was totally appropriate for the party, so I nodded my approval. "I love learning. I even like most of my classes, but I'm struggling because I can't take the classes that I want to. I can't explore what I'm interested in or get a degree in something that I love. It's just..." I sighed at the hopelessness of complaining. It wasn't going to do anything. "My father controls this part of my life. My mother controls basically all the others and the closer I get to graduation, the bigger this brick in my chest gets."

When her green eyes met my blue ones, there was nothing but sympathy in them. Her parents just wanted her to be happy. That was all that mattered to them, so she got to take whatever class she wanted without having to get them approved by her father.

"It's like I'm going to go my whole life without actually having any fun. And my father is smoking the devil's lettuce if he thinks that I'm going into politics. I couldn't imagine anything worse."

Kenzie shuddered when I mentioned going into politics. "Yeah. Gross. But I think I have the perfect solution." She dropped the dress on my bed and folded her arms under her breasts. "Road trip."

A smile played at my lips. "What?"

"Road trip. We hit the road and do something fun. No one will know or care."

I raised an eyebrow. "That should be a lot of fun with Donovan."

Her face fell because she knew as well as I did that he'd be right there with us.

Donovan was my full-time bodyguard and had been assigned to me in high school when my father had announced his plans to run for governor. Though, here at school, he was always there lurking but sometimes made sure to keep his distance. The Andersen family had a history that went further back than my father and they'd made a lot of enemies. The only reasonable solution to this to my father was for my brother and me to have body-guards to ensure we were protected. If we weren't with our parents, who had security of their own, then Donovan was with me and Mitch was with my brother.

I often wondered if either of them had a life and it took me two years to realize that they were the daytime security and switched out at night then another bodyguard, Sabian, took over on Donovan's days off.

Even if the shady way my family had made its money weren't enough, Dad had become governor and once his second term was up, he'd be running for senator. No one knew that part yet, but I was almost certain that he wanted to be president one day. I couldn't imagine the pressure and scrutiny my brother and I would be under then.

"Donovan isn't invited," she finally said. He was the reason I opted out of most parties.

Technically, he wasn't supposed to be my babysitter and was only supposed to make sure that I wasn't taken or hurt. Realistically, I knew part of his job was to report back to my parents everything I was doing. He'd tell my parents that I made a visit to Warner's office but it wasn't unusual to visit lots of people on campus. He wouldn't have known what we talked about.

"And where we would go?"

A giant smile spread across her face. "Forever 18 just started their tour and they have several dates in Michigan, then some in Ohio, Indiana, and Illinois. I think one in Wisconsin. I say we follow the tour. Make this a road trip. Stay gone as long as we want to. We might have to buy some tickets on Ticket Hub because they're sold out otherwise, but I don't care about the seats. I just want to be there."

"Hotels?"

"Yes. I'm not sleeping in your car."

Forever 18 was her jam. I knew them, obviously,

everyone did and they were good but I sure wasn't a superfan in the way Kenzie was.

The longer I thought about it, the more I was liking this idea. It might only be a week or two, but this sounded like more fun than I'd had in... maybe ever. This could be the one thing that I do for myself. Luckily, I had a bank account and credit card that my parents knew nothing about. I'd started that years ago with the allowance that they'd given me.

It never made sense. I got an allowance—more than some of my friends made at their part-time jobs —but was never allowed to go anywhere to use it. There was also all the money I'd technically inherited from my grandpa when I'd turned twenty-one but under the management of my parents until I graduate college. It'd only been a few months and I hadn't touched it, mostly because I didn't want it and was worried that my parents would be alerted if I withdrew any. Not to mention, I'd have to go through my dad to get it.

Yeah, I'd stay away from that for this trip and just use my savings.

"When do we leave?"

3

LONDON

"What's your problem?" Grayson asked me when we were the only two still awake on the bus. It happened that way sometimes.

Grayson and I had been friends for decades, which meant we knew most things about each other. You could never say you knew *everything* about someone, but Grayson was as much a brother to me as my own actual brothers. There'd been three of us born into my family. All boys. And Grayson and I had always been together, so my parents claimed him as an honorary member, as his did me.

"I don't have a problem." I tipped my beer back against my lips.

"Oh, you do." He dropped onto the couch beside me.

"Nah. I'm tired. That's about it," I said. Grayson didn't say anything, but he watched me until I started talking again. "This shit just gets old fast."

"What shit."

"I love being on tour. You know that." I took another drink before continuing. Talking about feelings wasn't the easiest for me, even with Grayson. "But the grind gets old quick. Drive to the venue, set up, interviews, perform, leave. Rinse and repeat."

"Yeah, it does." He let out a yawn and ran his hands through his already messed-up hair and I could've guessed how his hair had gotten messed up now that Lilah was a permanent fixture on our bus. It could've been worse. At least we all got along. "It helps to have someone to pass the time with."

"I have you."

Grayson snorted. "I meant someone to pass the time with in a *fun* way. Listen." He turned himself so that he was facing me. "You and I are always going to be friends. I'll always be here for you, but have you considered—"

"Knock it off." Where he was headed with that was somewhere I didn't want to go.

Hadn't wanted to go since high school.

"I'm just saying that since Holly—"

My jaw tightened and I squeezed the bottle in my hand so tightly that I thought it might break. "Don't fuckin' go there. I'm over that."

"Sure you are." Grayson pushed to his feet and drained his bottle. "I'm going to bed."

Then I was alone again, which was how I preferred it when my thoughts were all fucked-up unless I was balls-deep in a woman, but we had to leave the venue so quickly tonight, that wasn't a possibility.

I'd never get caught up in a woman the way Grayson was with Lilah. I loved it for them, but that life wasn't for me. That decision had been made a long time ago.

Sometime much later, I shuffled back to my bunk and fell asleep. The bus was excellent to sleep on with its rocking motion.

A few days later, I felt a lot better. Or rather, there'd been a couple of women who'd made me feel better. My mother had warned me not to get caught up in the lifestyle, but in this case, everyone knew what was up. The women knew it was a one-night thing and I knew it was a one-night thing.

It worked for me and I was respectful. Everyone left happy.

We were getting ready for our show, which was basically sold out, our manager Sean had told us. We loved being sold out, no matter the size of the venue. Part of performing was feeding off the energy of the crowd and when it was sold out, or almost sold out, it was so easy to get pumped up.

Jamison and Thatcher were plotting something in the corner, but at least they were ready for the show. That wasn't always a guarantee. Grayson was running through his pre-show hydration because singing wasn't easy on the vocal cords. Had to be hydrated.

Lennox and I were still shirtless and getting ready.

"So who's next?" Lennox asked as if any of us knew what he was referring to.

Becca and Lilah came through the door with some clothes for us. They always had backups in the room in case something happened. Usually, the stylists were set up earlier, but sometimes, they came in just before the show started because as Lilah put it, our vibe changed day to day.

Sometimes hour to hour.

"Next for what?" I asked as I watched Lilah and Becca head directly to the corner where the clothes stands were.

Those two women had gotten good at pretending they couldn't hear our conversations, though they didn't need to do that, given that none of us gave a fuck about what they heard.

"To get pussy-whipped like Grayson," Jamison answered.

"Watch it," Grayson warned though I could see Lilah holding back a laugh.

I wouldn't have characterized Grayson quite that way, but it was fun that Jamison had.

Grayson and Lilah had real feelings for each other. Feelings that once in a while I'd get a small pang of jealousy over. Then I'd remind myself what it had been like with Holly and any thoughts of a relationship were wiped clean from my brain.

"My guess is Jamison," I told them, which got me a horrified look from the man in question.

"You're so fucking wrong." He pushed up from his chair. "My guess is you, London, and not because you just tried to pin it on me, but I have a feeling about you. You're going to find some woman who makes your heart go pitter-patter and it'll be done."

Becca turned around and took a step toward us. "Can I ask why you guys are talking about falling in love the same way most people talk about getting chlamydia?"

A low rumble of laughter spread through the room. The thing I loved most about Becca was that she never held back. She was professional, but since we'd all become friends, she didn't hold back.

"Because it's the same thing," Jamison told her. "For me, fucking one woman for the rest of my life *is* an STI."

The rest of us didn't hold back how funny we thought that all was. Though I'd decided to stay out of that conversation with Becca. There were things that I didn't want to talk about.

Instead, I focused on picking a shirt for tonight. As they continued to talk, Lilah quietly helped me choose the right one.

"You're awful." Becca shook her head at Jamison.

"Of course he is," Thatcher told her. "And that's not a new thing. Jamison has been that way since he started having sex. Even in high school."

"But why?" she pushed. "Why wouldn't you want one woman with whom you could spend the rest of your life?"

"Becca," Lilah said with a sigh, but her best friend waved her off. Lilah glanced at Grayson across the room and shrugged and he gave her a small grin.

Those two were fucking perfect for each other.

Becca turned to me. "What about you?"

"What about me?" I asked though I knew exactly what she meant.

"Are you like the other Neanderthals who think falling in love is akin to being shot in the head?"

"Yup." I kept busy by pulling my shirt over my head, hoping that it would deter any further questions.

"Of course he is," Lennox added. "London might even be the king of seeking strange. He never even fucks the same girl twice."

"Not true," I told him. "Sometimes I don't remember them from the first time."

Becca made a gagging noise, which had been what I was going for. It wasn't true. I remembered them as far as I knew, but I wanted off this topic and onto something else. Immediately.

"You guys are so fucking gross." But at least Becca turned back to Lilah and continued their work.

As the music from the venue came to an end, we knew we only had a short while before we'd head on stage. Our opening act, Westland, was good and the crowd always loved them. This arrangement was working out well.

"You OK?" Grayson asked me quietly as we all

finished up the last of the things we did before the show and headed out to the hallway.

"Of course." I glanced at him then straight out in front of me. "That shit doesn't bother me. You know that." I'd turned my feelings off a long time ago.

"I just thought—"

"Nah. I'm good. No worries."

Then it was time. The five of us took the stage and settled into whatever instrument we played. The place was black with only the flashing of some cameras. What a waste. They wouldn't get anything because it was too dark. They couldn't see us. Maybe some shadows, but that could've been anyone.

As I played songs that I could've played in my sleep, my thoughts began to wander.

Grayson hadn't been all wrong the other night. The constant random women did get tiring some-times. Like I still fucked them when I wanted to and they were more than ready to, but sometimes, it took a lot of effort.

There was no way I wanted a relationship again, no way I wanted to love someone with all of my heart again, but the hookups weren't all that enticing anymore. I knew that Grayson had been getting rest-less before he'd met Lilah. Hell, he'd stopped doing half the stuff he'd been doing before, so it hadn't been hard to see. Now that I was feeling a little restless, people were going to think I was headed in the same direction.

No fucking way.

It was more me being... desensitized, I guess. Like if you watch a lot of porn, eventually, you were going to need crazier porn to get you off. In my case, fuck a lot of women, and just having an accessible vagina was no longer exciting.

After the show, we were all back in the hotel. Our next show wasn't far, so we got to stay in a hotel for the night and would travel the few hours tomorrow. I loved nights in the hotel, but tonight, I went right to bed. I didn't want the inquisition to start again because I didn't talk about Holly ever. Period.

And even though I could hear laughter from Jamison's room next to mine, I didn't regret my decision at all.

In fact, I was the first one awake the next morning. I'd taken a shower and packed up my small bag and was down in the lobby grabbing a bagel and coffee from the little snack bar in the lobby. There were tables available, so I grabbed one to enjoy my time alone until Sean dropped into the seat across from me.

That man was a big guy. The kind you wouldn't

want to fuck with in a dark alley. He was as tall as the rest of us with dark blond hair and dark eyes but he had a bigger muscle content. The rest of us were muscular but they were lean muscle. Only a little bulge. Sean was big without being ridiculous.

"You're up early," he said before taking a drink of his coffee.

"Went to bed early. When are we leaving?"

He glanced at his phone then back to me. "Supposed to be in about twenty minutes, but you know how that goes."

"I do. That's why you tell us about an hour before we have to actually leave."

He closed his eyes and took a breath. "Did the rest of the guys figure that out?"

"No. They just think they're always late."

"Good," he said with a nod. "If they do know they're not actually late, they'll start really *being* late, thinking they have a lot of spare time. At least Grayson is always on time now that he's with Lilah."

"Yeah. Probably can't sleep through her getting ready and I don't think that woman has ever been late for anything in her life."

"Probably not." He chuckled. "Maybe Grayson doesn't *want* to sleep through her getting ready."

That part was probably true. And we both knew why.

Sean and I talked about the tour and some other things as we finished up our breakfast. Surprisingly, everyone joined us as we were tossing our trash. Usually, Sean was waiting on someone.

We were on the road and headed to the next venue in Ohio, though none of us had family coming to the show. Sometimes they did when we were close to Michigan, but I thought they were just waiting for the show in Detroit.

The scenery was boring as it flew past us, and the guys were all rather quiet. Thatcher and Jamison were playing on the PlayStation, while Grayson, Becca, and Lilah were in the back. I had no idea what they were doing. I was strumming my guitar, trying to figure out this melody I had in my head and Lennox went back to sleep in his bunk. Or that was what he *said* he was doing.

Some buses had a big bedroom at the back of the bus, as big as you could get in confined spaces, but ours was more of a lounge area. There were couches back there and a television. In the corner, we had a weight set stashed away because sometimes on the long drives, one of us wanted to get in some exercise.

I was glancing around and looked out the front

window when the bus slowed due to traffic. We didn't have the divider up right now.

It looked like everyone had slowed down to pass a car that had broken down on the side of the high-way. There were two women outside the car, one talking animatedly, the other shaking her head.

The one shaking her head was fucking striking. Hair over her shoulders looked like champagne cascading down. She was short, for sure, with curves in all the right places. Fucking gorgeous from what I could tell and the thought of those two standing on the side of the road didn't sit well with me.

"They probably have help on the way, right?" I asked the guys.

Thatcher hit the *pause* button on his game to look for himself. "I'm not sure. Cell reception is spotty right now, but it's there."

"Should we stop? Help them?" I asked. If I'd had a sister and she was broken down on the side of a highway, I'd hope that someone would help. Someone who wasn't going to hurt them because two young women on the side of the road wasn't the safest situation.

"I'm sure they've got someone else to help," Jamison said, then he nudged Thatcher to get the game going.

"We should stop to make sure."

"Make sure what?" Grayson was suddenly out in the main area with us. He hadn't been there a minute before.

"Make sure those women are OK," I said. We hadn't reached them yet, traffic was crawling, but we were close enough to see what was happening.

"Yeah, that won't be weird," he told me. "A bunch of guys getting off a bus to approach them."

"First." I pushed to my feet. "It's possible they'll recognize us. Second, we have Becca and Lilah with us. Third, it's not like I'm saying we should take them on the bus. I'm just saying we shouldn't leave them on the side of the road without asking if they have help on the way."

After thinking about it for a moment, Grayson nodded. "Yeah. OK. You're right. Hey, Kelly," he called a little louder. "Can you pull off when it's safe so we can see if those women need some help?"

"Will do," our driver called back.

The women watched us warily as Kelly got us off the road and put the bus's hazards on.

I was the first one off the bus and to the women, but I knew at least Grayson was behind me. We didn't need all five of us right away and that might've scared them anyway.

The woman with her arms wrapped around herself, like she was trying to make herself smaller, now had her blonde hair pulled up into a bun and sad, blue eyes. She was already small. Why she'd make herself smaller was the question.

She didn't talk, though. It was her friend, a woman with wild, auburn hair and piercing green eyes, who stepped in front of me.

I settled my focus on her, though the blonde had me asking so many questions that I'd never get the answer to. "Is there anything we can do to help?" I asked.

The last thing I was going to do is leave a couple of women on their own on the side of the road.

Anything could've happened.

4

CHARLOTTE

Somehow, I managed to get us a three-hour head start before Donovan would notice me missing. It took perfect planning and a few tiny lies about still having an exam to do, though, if my bodyguard had paid any attention, he'd know that exams had ended days ago.

I'd told him that I had one last one that was three hours long. He shadowed me until I entered the building, though he never came into class with me. Usually, he was outside the class or outside the building. Today, it was the building probably because it was such a beautiful day outside.

After going inside, I kept walking right out the door on the other side. I'd never tried to slip away from any security before, so they wouldn't have had any reason to suspect.

Out the back door and over to the parking lot, I hopped into Kenzie's car. My suitcase was already in the trunk, thanks to Kenzie's sly moves of getting it there while I was tricking my bodyguard. We were on our road trip headed to Ohio for the first of many Forever 18 concerts. The band might've been Kenzie's obsession, but they were good and I was a fan.

"I can't believe we pulled this off," Kenzie said before she squealed.

We'd been friends for a long time and though I knew security annoyed her, she never complained if I couldn't do something or go somewhere without a shadow. In fact, she'd started to see if she could get a reaction out of them, but so far, she hadn't.

One time, she'd pushed a male friend of ours at me and acted scandalized as if we were doing something we shouldn't have been. It didn't work. It never worked with stuff like that.

"I know," I told her. "But remember, he'll know something is up as soon as that exam is supposed to be over, so we only have three hours to put as much distance between us and them."

"Your phone?"

"I have it, but it's off so my dad can't track us. If we want to do the whole week."

"Right. Dire emergency only."

"Exactly."

Kenzie was the only person who knew that there was a tracking app on my phone. It was ridiculous. I was a grown woman who shouldn't have been watched by her father, but if I wanted this education, I'd have to follow his rules. Besides, I'd rather know what he was doing than have him sneak around about it. Without him and my mom, I wouldn't even have the phone. With no job to pay for it, this was the best way out that I could figure. Not to mention if I got my own plan, my father would be convinced I'm hiding something and lose his shit.

"I can't believe we're actually doing this." The excitement running through me was intense, given that I'd never done anything like this before. Normally, I played my father's game because it was easier.

"You know people do this all the time. Go to another state for a concert."

"Yes." That didn't dash the feeling of freedom spreading through me. Maybe for this one week, I'd see what it was like to be normal. "I do know that, in theory, but I don't *really* know that. And eventually, I have to call my brother."

"No way, Charlotte. We're rebels this week." Kenzie got us away from school quickly and onto the highway. There was a sense of urgency, even though we both knew we had some time. "No calling your family."

"I have to, Kenzie. I have to call my brother. Eventually, the alarm is going to be sounded and I don't want him or my mom thinking I'm dead in a ditch somewhere or my father thinking someone took me because he's so controversial and wants to be president. There's no telling what his reaction would be."

A half-smile formed on her face. "Because he loves his little girl so much?"

I snorted at the ridiculousness of her statement. "Not hardly. Because he wouldn't want anyone getting the upper hand on him. Or embarrassing him. Or showing him up. You know how he is."

"That, I do."

"And my brother is the safest option. He'll make sure they know I'm OK, but even if he knows where I am, which he won't, he'd never tell them. He might play the game some too, but he's the one who's been telling me to tell my dad to fuck off for years. But he still knows why I can't just yet."

"OK. Fine, but you'll use my phone to do it and keep it short in case your dad is tracing the call."

A giggle bubbled up from my chest. "I don't think he's monitoring it like that, but I'm not turning my phone on unless our lives are at stake."

She nodded in agreement then focused back on the road.

We'd been driving a few hours when it happened. There was a noise, a clunk, and smoke began billowing out from under the hook then the wheel started shaking. Kenzie had to coast us off to the side of the road.

"What the hell was that?" she asked, out of breath, as if she'd been struggling with a giant whale.

"I don't know, but we should get out of the car." I pointed out the windshield to the smoke.

Only it wasn't smoke, but steam.

Kenzie popped the hood and got it open, as if she knew what to look for. The moment it opened, she jumped back due to the amount of steam.

"Shit," she muttered.

The two of us walked to the back of the car, sure to stay away from the busy highway. It was only a two-lane road in each direction, but there was constant traffic and they were moving. This fun trip wasn't going to land with one of us getting squashed.

"I guess I'll call a tow truck." Kenzie pulled out her phone then walked away. After a second, she moved to another location, then another.

"What's going on?" I followed her.

"It's not placing my call. Please don't tell me that we broke down in the last place in America that doesn't have cell coverage."

I snorted. "It's just a dead spot. We could walk a bit until we get service."

"Who knows how far that will be?"

That was true. There was another option that was pretty unappealing to me, but it might be our only one. "I could try my phone."

"No way. You know that as soon as you do, we have to go back. Do you want to go back?"

I shook my head. "No."

"And besides, it probably won't work anyway." She wasn't wrong. If she didn't have service, then I wouldn't have it, either.

"So what are we going to do?"

The silence between us became uncomfortable only because it showed that neither of us had any idea of what to do. Without a phone, there wasn't much we *could* do.

And there went our head start.

My stomach tightened at the thought of Donovan finding us or one of my father's goons. Donovan was nice enough, but not every part of my father's security was. Maybe they needed to be assholes. I didn't know.

The family I'd been born into wasn't normal to begin with and I didn't want to know half the things they were involved with.

We were throwing out the worst ideas when a huge bus pulled over in front of our car.

"This is when we're murdered," I whispered to make her laugh.

"Yeah. Kidnapped and murdered by someone on a huge fucking bus. It's so incognito."

A tall man with messy, brown hair stepped off the bus wearing jeans and a blue T-shirt. Lean, muscles corded his arms and as he got closer, we could see the veins that popped off his skin. I didn't know why Kenzie and I liked the veins, and certainly there could've been too much, but with him, there wasn't.

Another man with dark hair followed the first and I wasn't sure whether we should've been scared or turned on. They were both incredibly good-looking and somehow familiar. But it was the second man that held my attention. I'd never seen someone as beautiful as him in my life. He was exactly my type, if I'd looked around enough to develop one. Everything about him had my heart beating a little hard and my breath coming a little faster.

If I didn't get my shit together, I was going to embarrass myself.

"Holy shit," Kenzie whispered as if she could read my mind.

I gave her a questioning look, but she didn't have time to answer before they got to us.

"Is there anything we can do to help?" the first man asked once he'd come to a stop. The second stood beside him.

"I don't think so," Kenzie told him. "I think this thing is DOA." She tried to lean back against the trunk of the car but missed, instead plummeting to the ground until I grabbed her to stop the impact.

"Shit," she muttered but I could barely keep from laughing. These guys were hot, that was obvious, but her nervousness was out of control.

"Let me take a look," the second one offered as he took tried to keep a smile at bay. But he looked so sexy doing it. "I don't know a lot about cars, but I know a little."

The two of us stepped aside so he could get through, but Kenzie grabbed my wrist and held on, squeezing a little too roughly.

"You're going to leave a bruise," I told her quietly so she'd at least loosen up a bit. "What's wrong with you?"

Again, she didn't get to respond before they were back in front of us.

"There's a giant hole in your radiator," the second man explained. "Did you hit something?"

"Not that I know of," Kenzie responded.

"Well, you definitely won't be able to drive it. Did you call a tow truck?"

Kenzie shook her head quickly but didn't speak, so I did. "There's no cell service. We were thinking about walking to the next exit."

"We can't let you do that," the first man said. "Walking on the highway is dangerous. We can give you a ride."

I raised my eyebrows because the last thing I was going to do was get on a bus with a couple of strange men. Not a chance.

"I'm Grayson, by the way." The second man held his hand to his chest. "This is London."

And then I completely understood both why they looked familiar and why Kenzie was shutting off the blood flow to my hand again.

I understood the reason she was holding my hand so tightly. We both knew who they were but being famous didn't mean it was safe to get on that bus with them. It's still taking a ride from strangers.

"We can't do that," I told him.

"Why not?" London asked.

"Because two young women getting on a bus with two strangers is a situation you see on the news," I said. London snorted. "With a banner reading, 'Have you seen these women?' No way."

"Charlotte..." Kenzie whispered then turned to them. "We know who you are. We're fans."

"They're still strangers." There was no way around that fact. Were they likely rapists and murderers? No. Probably not, but years of having it drilled into my head that danger lurked around every corner wasn't going to go away too quickly.

"It's not just us," Grayson explained. "The rest of the guys are on there."

"That doesn't really make it sound better."

"My girlfriend is also on there and her best friend."

As if on cue, two women stepped off the bus. One with hair that resembled liquid chocolate and the other with blonde hair like mine. Maybe a bit lighter.

They came bouncing over to us.

"Everything OK?" the brunette asked.

"Car broke down," I told her. "They've offered us a ride to the next exit, but I explained that us getting on a bus with a bunch of guys wasn't exactly the best idea."

"No kidding." She glanced at Grayson and from the way they looked at each other, I had to assume this was the girlfriend. "I don't know if this will help, but I'm Lilah and this is my best friend, Becca. We're on the bus as well. It's safe."

"Charlotte," she whispered.

I glanced at Kenzie and swallowed hard. "I'm not entirely sure we have a choice. We could ride with them to the next exit or ride with the truck driver when he gets here."

"True," she agreed, then she sighed. "This sucks so bad."

"I promise it's not that bad," London told her with a smirk.

"Not that," I explained. "We were headed to your concert tonight and now... who knows? It's not like we can call anyone for help, so we'll be stuck at the garage until they fix it. Or in a hotel until they fix it. This was our end of the semester celebration."

"Come with us," Becca offered with excitement. "Instead of going to the next exit, come to the show with us. We could call someone for your car, but you can ride with us."

London turned to her with a not-so-friendly look.

"What?" she asked. "Is that a problem? It's literally only like another hour."

"No," he relented. "It's not a problem."

"We have to get our bags from the car," Kenzie said the squealed, more to me than them. "But I think we should do it. At least this way, we'll get one show out of it." Then out of the side of her mouth, she added, "Not to mention ride with the freaking band."

I paused and ran over all the scenarios in my head. None of them were better than this and the longer we stood out there discussing it, the closer Donovan would get to finding us.

"OK," I finally agreed. "Let's get our stuff."

"We can call for a truck once we have service again."

"Yeah," I agreed as Kenzie and I were walking

away. "We'll leave a note, too. You know they're going to find it."

I didn't miss the way his brows furrowed, but I also wasn't going to explain any further.

Right now, this adventure was for Kenzie and me.

5
—————

LONDON

Well, I'd been thinking that I wanted something different to happen, something surprising, and I guess I'd gotten what I'd wanted.

Charlotte and her friend headed back to the car to get their bags. I only knew the blonde's name because her friend had said it. And for some reason, I couldn't take my eyes off her as she made her way back to the car in the short sundress with her hair brushing across her back.

No. I was *not* going to try to fuck this woman. Either of them. We were just giving them a ride... to the venue, apparently. At least they liked our music. I couldn't imagine being on the bus with a couple of people who hated it and wanted to let us know—

because those people *were* out there. Fine. Don't like our music, but why feel the need to be loud about it?

"Is this a good idea?" Grayson asked.

"You'd rather leave them on the side of the road?" Lilah countered.

"Of course not. But they could be crazy. We don't know them."

She snorted. "They're more at risk than you are. They weren't freaking out or anything and they don't know you, even if they know *of* you."

"That's true," I agreed. "What do you think she meant about the car?"

"What?" Grayson asked.

"She said they'll find it. What the fuck does that mean?"

"No idea. It's weird, though. Maybe she means like the cops who will probably have it towed or something."

"Yeah. Maybe."

They were damsels in distress and we got to play the hero. Though it was riskier for them. We wouldn't hurt them, but they didn't know that. I supposed having Lilah and Becca around made them feel a little safer.

Charlotte and her friend came back, each with a single bag and a purse strapped across their chests.

They were chatting and by the serious looks on their faces, they weren't chatting about how much fun this was going to be.

"I'm Lilah," she said once we were headed back to the bus. "This is Becca. Those two introduced themselves already, yes?"

"Yes. I'm Charlotte. This is Kenzie."

Introductions happened again once we were on the bus. Given the wide eyes with mouths slightly open, Thatcher, Jamison, and Lennox hadn't expected us to come back with the women we'd stopped to help, but being as laid-back as we all were, they didn't argue it.

Instead, the four women sat around the table while us guys scattered around the couch, the chair, and even the floor in Jamison's case. I was on the couch closest to the table and every time Charlotte glanced at me with those deep-blue eyes, it was like a punch to the gut. Only I didn't understand it.

"Since we've got like an hour or so, how about you guys tell us what it's like to be rock stars?" Kenzie had been the quietest when we'd been on the side of the highway but now seemed to have come out of her shell.

"It's fucking amazing, of course," Jamison

answered before anyone else could, though I noticed Lilah roll her eyes.

"Do either of you want a drink?" she asked before the rest of us could give an answer. "It was hot out there."

"I could use a water," Charlotte said quietly and Kenzie agreed.

While Lilah got them settled with that, I decided to answer the question that had been asked. "Being on the road sucks sometimes. It's fucking fantastic others. I think it's like any other job, where there are pros and cons, but I wouldn't trade it for anything."

Charlotte turned slightly in her seat with her eyes narrowed. "You think being legitimate *rock stars* is like any other job?"

"Well, not the job itself, but there are good things and bad things, absolutely."

She considered me for a minute before focusing on the conversation around us. I contributed when it was right and pretty quickly we all forgot that Charlotte and Kenzie were strangers. Maybe they hadn't. I wouldn't know that, but the rest of us were comfortable and they sure seemed like it.

"Were you planning on heading back after the show tonight?" Becca asked the women. "Oh, wait. Where are you from?"

"We were driving down from Ann Arbor. That's where we go to school." Kenzie took a drink of her water before continuing. "And no. We weren't planning on driving back tonight. We were going to find a hotel." She tucked a piece of hair behind her ear then glanced at Charlotte. Charlotte let out a deep sigh.

"I don't think Kenzie wants to admit this because it might make us sound like stalkers." Charlotte glanced at me, making my stomach tighten. "But we had plans to basically go to as many of the shows this week as we could. It was a last-minute thing because I wanted to do something fun. Have a little freedom."

I hated the sound of that. "You don't have freedom?"

Those deep-blue eyes met mine and if I'd known her better, I would've said sadness clouded them. "Not the way I'd like to."

"Why not?" I prodded. It took Grayson slapping my shoulder for me to realize that I was prying into this woman's life and I didn't even know her.

"You can still go to the shows, right?" Lilah asked.

Charlotte sighed. "Not if we don't have a ride. And renting a car wasn't really part of the plan."

The feeling in the air changed at that.

"You could tag along with us," Grayson offered, bringing a scowl from Jamison and a groan from Thatcher. "What? We have the room."

"How am I supposed to bring women back here when there are so many women already here?" Jamison had a point, but that hadn't crossed my mind at all. The rest of us chuckled, but Charlotte turned fully in her seat to face him.

"Do you think Kenzie or I would cockblock you? I'm crushed."

Now we all laughed again and Becca gave her a high five.

Yes, we brought women back to the bus sometimes, but not as often as most people thought, given that we were always on our way somewhere else. It was more likely for us to hook up backstage before we headed out. Having them on the bus could get tricky. What if the driver pulled out and she was still there? That was messy.

"I think it's a great idea," Lilah countered. "It'd be nice to even out the testosterone around here for a little while."

Kenzie bit her lips together like she was trying to hold in her excitement. Charlotte glanced at me, then back to her friend.

"If we can have the assurance that no one's going

to bury us in a shallow grave, then I think it'd be OK. At least until they catch up. Even then, you could stay, Kenzie." It was like Charlotte had forgotten that there were other people around her. That was twice she'd mentioned "they" and now I wanted to know exactly who she was talking about. I wouldn't ask, but I wanted to know.

Luckily, I didn't have to.

"Who are 'they'?" Becca asked and I didn't doubt everyone else wanted to know, too.

I cringed at the idea of explaining anything. "My parents. It's nothing."

Didn't sound like nothing. Kenzie and Charlotte looked to be around Lilah and Becca's age. Maybe a few years younger, but they had to be in college, which meant she couldn't be a runaway.

Fuck. What if she *was* a runaway? I had to ask.

"You said you go to school in Ann Arbor? College?"

"Yes," Charlotte answered. "Just finished our third year, so no, you aren't contributing to the delinquency of minors or anything. We didn't run away. We were getting away for a bit."

Yet that didn't answer the question I really wanted to know. Why was she worried about someone finding her? Why would they have fun on our bus until her parents caught up to her if she was a grown-ass adult?

I didn't think I was going to get the answers in front of everyone, so I didn't ask.

That didn't stop me from being determined to find out.

We were getting close to the arena when Thatcher asked if we were stopping for something to eat or eating at the venue. Given that we now had guests, we agreed to stop for food.

"It has to be relatively quick," Grayson said as we all got off the bus in the parking lot of a Denny's. At least we knew everyone could find something they liked here. "We have to get to the venue for soundcheck."

"We know, Mom." Jamison gave him a thumbs-up, making the women giggle.

The waitress was happy to accommodate us once we were inside by putting a few tables together so we'd have room. I ended up across from Charlotte with everyone else scattered about.

There was something about her that I couldn't put my finger on. She was beautiful, obviously, but it was the way she looked at me like she could see through everything else to my real thoughts and feelings. It was unnerving. I didn't want anyone to see those things. They were just for me.

Yet I could easily fucking imagine fisting my hand into her hair and claiming that mouth.

No, London, I told myself, like I was chastising a dog.

I probably shouldn't have been thinking the thoughts I was about her, but I couldn't help it. The way her fingers brushed across her bottom lip when she was listening to someone else and the easy smile she'd give... There was an innocence about her. An innocence that I wanted to be the one to chase away.

It was a perfect idea, really. She was here only for a limited time, my favorite kind of woman. I could answer all my own questions about her innocence, then she'd be gone tomorrow.

Yet somehow, this time, it felt wrong.

Charlotte leaned over to her friend and whispered, "I'm going to run to the restroom." We'd already ordered, so now all we had to do is wait.

"Oh, me too." Kenzie jumped to her feet and the two of them walked away.

"You should probably stop looking at her like that," Grayson told me. The combination of his low voice and the chatter around us made it so that no one else would probably hear him.

"Looking at who like what?"

One corner of his mouth rose in a smirk like he knew I knew exactly what he was talking about. "Looking at Charlotte like you want to taste her."

Fuck. I *did* want to taste her. There were just some people you were intensely attracted to, even though you didn't know them. I couldn't do anything about it.

"I'm not looking at her like that."

"Yeah, you are," Jamison added from the chair that would've been beside Kenzie on the other side of the table.

There went any hope of no one else hearing Grayson.

"You can both fuck off."

The two of them chuckled, but thankfully, either no one else was interested in this conversation or they couldn't hear it.

"We could, but we won't."

"Seriously." Grayson leaned in closer and dropped his voice lower. "You look like you want to eat her and while I'm not one to discourage that— after all, a man needs what he needs—it's pretty obvious to anyone who looks at you. Probably including her. Don't make her feel uncomfortable."

"I haven't *done* anything!"

He held up a hand to stop me. "You haven't. But eventually, she's going to see how you're looking at her and it will make her uncomfortable. Let's not do that." He sat back in his chair, then added, "Especially since I have a feeling that Lilah and Becca are going to want them to stay with us for the week that they were planning to go to the shows."

"What?" That couldn't happen. Hell. I'd rent them a car to get them off my bus.

"Women are weird. It's like they're already best friends or some shit."

The way the four of them had sat around the table on the bus giggling flashed through my mind.

He wasn't kidding. It was like they were all best friends already and I didn't do complicated. Fucking Charlotte when she was on my bus for a week would be the definition of complicated. That would give the illusion that I was up for a relationship, which I fucking was not.

It'd be best to stay clear of her. All I had to do was convince my uncomfortably hard dick that this was the best way to handle it.

6

CHARLOTTE

When the bus stopped at a Denny's for something to eat, I praised the universe.

I hadn't eaten all day. Not even before I'd left for my fake exam. My stomach had been turning at the thought of what we'd been about to do. Now that we were doing it, had actually ditched Kenzie's car and were now on a bus that they wouldn't even think of tracking, I was starving.

But first, the restroom.

I'd let Kenzie know that I was headed there and she of course wanted to come with me. We hadn't had a moment alone since the bus had shown up on the side of the road. A little chatting between the two of us was a good idea. To make sure we were both on the same page and neither felt uncomfortable.

"Holy shit," she said as soon as we got into the restroom and the door had closed. "Can you believe this, Charlotte? Forever 18 are our knights in shining armor?"

I held up a hand. "I wouldn't go that far. They really just did what every other person who passed us should have."

"But they *did it*. Now we're on their bus." She went into one stall and I into the other. There was a reason I'd come to the restroom. "Like we're friends or something."

"Again. I wouldn't go that far. They're helping us out and that's nice. But I think that's about it."

She groaned then flushed her toilet before going back out of her stall. I followed right behind and we started washing our hands in sinks side by side. "You're only saying that because you're used to meeting famous people because of your dad."

"I mean... they're people. Plus every single once I've met with my parents as been an asshole."

"But come on." Her hand was still wet when she grabbed my wrist. "This is cool, right?"

Fighting back a laugh so I didn't give into her too quickly, I said, "I guess it's pretty cool."

As we dried our hands, we kept talking until she let out a squeal that threatened to burst my eardrum.

"What?" I asked, thinking that something was really wrong.

"Just everything. This whole situation." Her voice echoed around the tiny restroom.

"You know this place echoes, right?"

"Yes."

"So they can probably hear you out there."

Her eyes widened and her mouth fell open. "Shit. I'll stop doing that."

I turned to leave, but her hand, now dry, grabbed my wrist again.

"You see the way that London is looking at you, right?"

My stomach clenched. If he knew who I was, that could've changed things. Weirder things have happened than a strange guy knowing who my father was then taking pictures or something that would eventually get me into trouble. "What? Looking at me how?"

"Like he wants to eat you with a spoon."

This time, it was my laugh that echoed. "You're crazy."

"Am not. Pay attention, woman," she said. I shook my head and left the restroom with her. Right before we got back to the table, she whispered, "We talked about freedom. What would be more freeing than a one-night stand with a fucking rock star?"

My cheeks heated with her words. As my best friend, Kenzie knew that I'd never had a one-night stand in my life. She knew how lame my entire history was. It was hard to do those things under the watchful eyes of my father's security.

Sometimes that made me feel like I was missing out on an important part of my young adulthood. Other times, it made me really think about my attitude toward sex. Which meant that I didn't know if I was a one-night stand kind of person. No shame to anyone who was. In fact, I envied Kenzie and her ability to let go with someone she barely knew enough for them both to get what they needed. I just had never been able to do that. Everything my parents had said to me over the years echoed in my brain every time I thought I might want to do it.

Every reminder of how my family had worked hard to change how they were seen. How one mistake could've deterred my father's political career. About how they'd know if I stepped out of line due to my babysitters. That was what I thought my security was. Babysitters. No one would kidnap me to get to my dad. That was just stupid. I wasn't anybody.

The entire group of us ate and talked, though Grayson reminded us that we couldn't lag. Soundcheck was right around the corner, not to mention that Lilah and Becca had to get the dressing room set up.

I loved the way he looked out for his girlfriend.

And I couldn't ignore the fact that Kenzie was absolutely wrong.

London wasn't attracted to me. He didn't want me, given the fact that he barely spared me a glance after I'd gotten back to the table.

After lunch, we went straight to the venue. I had no idea what Kenzie and I were going to do, but they said we could hang out there until showtime. The venue was ours to explore.

"Sean," Grayson yelled down a hallway once we were in the backstage area.

Kenzie was squeezing my hand the entire time to make sure she didn't explode with excitement. It was exciting once I got past all my hesitation and caution. No one could deny that. I supposed I showed it in a different way than her.

"What's up?" A man not quite twice my age, by the looks of it, approached the group. When he saw us, he added, "I don't remember you two being on the bus when it left Indianapolis."

"We weren't," I answered without thinking about it.

"Their car broke down. We gave them a ride." Grayson stepped forward to speak for the group

"Where are your seats?" Lilah looked back at the two of us.

"Nosebleeds," Kenzie told her. "This was kind of last minute." She dug in her purse then handed Lilah the confirmation, which had our seats on it.

Most places were doing digital tickets now, so we'd use her phone for actual admissions, but she'd printed the confirmation just in case something happened.

"Oh, yeah. These aren't great." She looked up at her boyfriend with those beautiful hazel eyes tinged with gold that I'd noticed earlier. They were unusual. At least to me.

"Is there something we can do about that, Sean?" Grayson handed the paper to the man I now assumed was their manager. It was the only thing that made sense.

"I'll take care of it." Then he looked to us. "I'm Sean, by the way. I manage these guys, so if there's anything you need while you're here, ask. Any friend of the guys is a friend of mine."

I didn't correct him. Kenzie and I weren't exactly friends of the guys, now were we? But I didn't know how these things worked and didn't ask.

As the band went to do soundcheck, leaving the four of us women in the hallway, Lilah turned to us. "Now that that's taken care of, why don't you two come with us? We don't expect you to do any of the work, but we can talk while Becca and I get the dressing room set up."

I nodded as Kenzie smiled, but I had so many questions. Still, we followed them into the dressing room. Those two told us to have a seat while they hung up some clothes and got out a steamer to get the wrinkles out.

The guys had to look their best, they said.

"What made you decide to follow Forever 18 for a week at the last minute?" Becca had her long, blonde hair pulled up into a bun.

"I had the tickets for Detroit since they went on sale though I didn't know if Charlotte would come with me," Kenzie explained. "But we were looking for something fun to do to celebrate the end of the semester."

"And this is what we came up with," I added.

Though we were supposed to be doing it on the cheap since I was using my secret savings account and it wasn't all that large. My inheritance should've all been mine to use, but it'd been put into an account that my father monitored and decided when to disperse as well as how much.

"I'm glad you did." Lilah put a shirt on the hanger carefully so as to not stretch out the neck. "I'm kind of glad your car broke down. We wouldn't have met you otherwise."

The four of us spent about an hour in that room talking as if we'd been friends our whole lives. I loved the way it worked when you just clicked with someone. It was the best feeling.

It was how Kenzie and I had become friends. She'd walked up to me at school years ago and told me that we were best friends now. We'd never looked back. I'd needed someone like her in my life. Someone who showed me that there was fun left in the world beyond all the duty.

The one who helped me stand up to my parents when it came to some of the little things like not wanting to date the assistant attorney general's son who was such a dude-bro that I wouldn't have been able to stand it.

The guys came back to the room, loud and boisterously laughing as if they'd just done something fun rather than their jobs. I couldn't imagine what it was like to have a job that you loved and found fun.

Kenzie and I tried to excuse ourselves, but Lilah insisted that it was fine for us to stay. The guys didn't care, but when London pulled his shirt over his head to start getting ready, I couldn't take my eyes off his chest and stomach. It was a thing of beauty. Something the likes of which I'd never seen in person, to be honest. Cut lines creating the abs without too much definition to make him look like he was flexing hard. Those side lines at the hip that I was told would form a V somewhere down below.

My best friend nudged me when I was staring like a creeper and that was what got me moving again. My ass was leaving that room when I mumbled some excuse.

"What are you doing?" she asked. "Besides drooling."

"I wasn't drooling," I snapped.

"You were kind of drooling and I wanted to be drooling, but you didn't wait to run out until after Thatcher had his shirt off. Now I don't know what I'm missing." Kenzie had always had a thing for bass players, which didn't make sense to me. Her personality said she should've been going for the drummer.

"I don't know." I shrugged. "I had to get out of there. Besides, the opening act is going to be starting soon."

After asking Sean if it was OK for us to just go through the backstage area or if we had to head around the venue, we made our way through the darkness to our seats. And they were fantastic seats.

The opening band was good, but Forever 18 was amazing. I now knew why Kenzie was obsessed. She'd seen them live before and ever since then, they'd been her favorite. I couldn't go with her that night. My father had had an event that I'd been required to attend.

My eyes kept drifting back to London and I tried to tell myself it was because he was on our side of the stage. But we were so close that it would've been easier to look across at Thatcher or Lennox. But no. My stupid eyes kept darting to him.

No one could say that London wasn't beautiful, for as much as a man could be "beautiful," but it was the way he carried himself and yes, the fact that it had been his idea to stop for us on the side of the road. That right there told me a lot about him as a person.

Once the show ended, we met Lilah and Becca back at the dressing room. Lilah said the guys had a meet and greet then would be in to take a shower. Normally, it was the other way around, but not tonight. She was cleaning up a bunch of the clothing when I realized that I hadn't called my brother yet.

"Can I use your phone?" I asked Kenzie because we both knew I couldn't use mine.

"Oh, shit. Now?"

I nodded. "I'm not going to call. Just text to let them know we're alive. They had to have found the car by now."

"True." She handed it over as we both tried to ignore the curiosity on the other women's faces. There were some secrets I wanted to keep for a little while. "Plus, we need to figure out what we're going to do next."

"What do you mean?" Lilah asked.

"Well..." I hit *send* on the text and handed the phone back to Kenzie. "You were all so nice to bring us here, but what do we do now? We were going to spend the night at a hotel and drive to the next show then spend a night there, then the next, etc. But now we need to rent a car and see if that's doable."

Again. The stupid money. I found it utterly funny that I was worried about money, given how much of it my family had. But that wasn't mine and I couldn't tap into the part that was, even if just having it made me feel a little dirty due to the way my family had come about it. It wasn't always through legal means.

"You should just go with us," Becca said excitedly. "We're driving to the next venue tonight because the guys have some radio spots to do in the morning. We'll sleep on the bus, but you'd have the day in Cincinnati. We could do something fun. The four of us."

"Just stay with us for the week," Lilah agreed. "No one will even notice."

"I don't know that we can do that." I glanced quickly at Kenzie, who was already pleading with her eyes. I *had* said I wanted something fun and different.

"I promise," Lilah assured us. "The guys won't care. There are extra bunks. You could share a bunk if that would make you feel better. It'd be so much fun."

Kenzie squeezed my arm and I was really going to need to train her to do something else when she was excited before I had permanent imprints of her fingers on my skin.

"If you're sure." It still felt like overstepping for me but it was a once-in-a-lifetime opportunity.

"We're sure." Those two said the words together, as if they'd planned it when I knew they hadn't.

Before we could make any more plans, the door opened and the guys all hurried in, talking a mile a minute. Their easy interaction made me smile.

Until I saw it.

The line of blood running down Jamison's arm.

I let out an almost inaudible gasp and slapped a hand over my face so I wouldn't puke. The blood drained from my face as my body got suddenly cold. The room was tilting slightly, even though I told myself it wasn't.

"Fuck," someone muttered.

"Oh, no." Kenzie put her hand on my back, but I barely felt it.

Suddenly, there was a large frame blocking my view of Jamison. "Come on." London kept his spot between the two of us as he led me out the door, then out of the venue.

The cool, night air hit me like a brick on, what felt like, my scorching skin. What a way to embarrass myself.

"Take some deep breaths," he ordered while gently running his hand up and down my back. It felt good and the fresh air chased away the iron smell of blood. I wasn't even sure if I was smelling Jamison's blood or if it was the memory of all the blood I'd smelled years ago. "You OK?"

I finally glanced up at him, my chest heaving in and out as I took in a breath and blew it out. "I'm OK."

"What the fuck happened in there?" He took a step back and right away, I missed the soothing nature of his hand on my back.

"I don't like blood."

7

LONDON

She didn't like blood. That had to be an understatement. In the dressing room, she'd looked like she'd been about to go down like a brick house. It had to be more than not liking the sight of blood and I wanted to know what it was. But I wouldn't push. Not yet.

"But you're OK now?"

She nodded. "What happened?"

"Jamison caught his arm on the corner of a shelf in the room where we were doing the meet and greet. It's not deep. Just a scratch, really."

"But there was so much..." She shivered. "Blood."

I furrowed my brows. There hadn't been. It was a scratch and a small trickle running down his arm.

He'd barely need a Band-Aid. "It wasn't a lot, Charlotte."

"It looked like a lot."

She crossed her arms over her stomach but ran her hands up and down the opposite arm like she was cold. I didn't have a sweatshirt or jacket to offer her, so I stepped closer and used my much larger hands to replace hers. I was hot as fuck, so if she needed some warmth, she could have mine.

"You're looking better," I said. She raised a brow, clearly doubting me, and I rolled my eyes. "Inside, you looked like all the blood had drained from your body. You don't look like that now."

"Good."

Our eyes locked with each other. The vulnerability in her eyes made me want to wrap my arms around her to make sure I was between her and the rest of the world. This was something more than not liking the sight of blood, but it wasn't my place to ask. And it sure as fuck wasn't my place to want to protect this woman.

She wasn't mine and I didn't want her to be. Though I had to remind myself several times in those few seconds that I would never fall in love again because Charlotte was the kind of woman a man could fall in love with. She wasn't a one-night stand. I didn't know how I knew this, but I fucking did.

"Do you want to go back in there?" I asked.

Her eyes watered at the corners as she bit down on her bottom lip and shook her head. "You can go, though. I'm fine out here."

"I'm not going to leave you alone in a dark at the back of the venue."

"There are lights." She pointed to the ones on the side of the building that barely gave off enough to see the ground.

I clenched my jaw together and shook my head. No way would I leave her out here alone.

"Don't you need to shower?" she asked.

To lighten the mood, I replied with, "Are you thinking about me naked?"

Her eyes widened slightly, but the tears dried up and that had been my goal. "Well, I *wasn't*." Which meant she was now and my cock began to harden in my jeans.

Fuck. Good thing she and Kenzie were about to go about their lives now.

"Lilah offered to let us ride on the bus with you the rest of the week."

Well, fuck me twice. "She did?"

Charlotte nodded. "But if it's a problem, we don't

have to. She only offered because we were going to head home and Lilah didn't want us to."

"Why would you head home?"

"Kenzie's car broke down and we'd have to rent one and that wasn't really in the budget for this trip."

Now my opinion had changed. I'd wanted her off the bus a moment ago, so I wouldn't try to fuck her. But now I wanted her *on* the bus because I didn't want to not see her anymore.

This was why I'd vowed not to have feelings for anyone again.

"I don't think that's a problem."

"What about the rest of the guys?"

I shook my head. "They won't care."

"If you're sure..."

"I am," I said way too quickly.

Charlotte looked up at me with those big, blue eyes and wet her bottom lip. That did nothing to help the situation growing in my jeans. I'd never gone for the "innocent" type, but fucking hell, it worked on Charlotte. All I could think about was just how innocent was she?

"Do you think they're done cleaning him up?"

It took me a full five seconds to realize that she was talking about Jamison, having forgotten what had brought us out here. "I'm sure they are. Let's go in. I'll check before you go into the dressing room."

"Thanks."

Once we were inside, I asked, "Why do you think your friend didn't come out to check on you?"

"She's used to me freaking out at the sight of blood. Plus, you took me out of there, so she'd know I wasn't alone. And..."

Her voice trailing off made me want to know more. "And?"

Shaking her head and rolling her eyes, Charlotte tried not to smile. "She thinks there's something between us. An attraction. She wouldn't want to get in the way of that." She looked up at me again as we slowly walked down the hallway. "Don't worry. I'm not going to jump you. I told her it was all in her head."

Fuck, I was in for the hardest week of my life.

The words were on the tip of my tongue, but I didn't say them. It definitely wasn't all in Kenzie's head for me, but maybe it was for her. I wasn't so full of myself that I thought it impossible for a woman to not be attracted to me. That would've been Jamison.

But now I wanted Charlotte so fucking badly that the idea of her not wanting me back didn't sit well.

Now that was messed up.

After a quick shower, I got dressed and headed to the bus. I was the last to arrive because I'd been outside with Charlotte while the others had done their thing. When I stepped on, I found that Jamison and Thatcher were nowhere to be seen, but since the bus had pulled out, I knew they were here somewhere. Kenzie was at the table with Becca, Lilah, and Grayson. The girls were eating a snack, but I couldn't make out what it was.

Charlotte was standing by the table in a pair of tiny shorts and a tank top that had to be her pajamas. All that exposed skin didn't help the fact that I wanted her. It made it worse. Her shirt was snug-fitting and she wasn't wearing a bra. Something I'd begun noticing about women when I was thirteen. Before that, I wouldn't have been able to tell who was wearing a bra and who wasn't. More than that, I wouldn't have cared.

Lennox was on the couch already playing the PlayStation.

One of Charlotte's arms was draped easily over her stomach and the other was bent like she was holding something in it and taking small bites. Her buttery-blonde hair hung over her shoulders, but the waves were mostly gone. She must've brushed it.

When she glanced over at me, I realized that I was staring like a fucking creeper.

"Want a snack?" Becca asked, but I waved her off, even though I could've eaten. Performing was hard work and I was always hungry after.

"I'll get something in a bit." I stopped as close to Charlotte as I dared. She was probably around five-four and I was six-one, so I towered over her.

"I think I'm going to head to bed," Kenzie announced. "It's been a long ass day."

"I'll come with you," Charlotte said to her, but she kept her eyes on me with a small grin until it was time for her to walk away.

Once the shade to their bunk shut, Grayson let out a low whistle. "Wow."

"Wow what?" I pulled the fridge open and snagged a container of grapes.

"You seriously want me to say it? They can hear out here, you know."

No. I didn't want him to say shit. Instead a ran a hand over my face and groaned.

A few hours later, I couldn't sleep, so I dropped quietly out of my bunk and went to the main area with my guitar in hand. I'd play quietly, but I'd play. It helped me when I couldn't sleep. But I also wasn't alone.

"Looks like someone's catching feelings," Jamison told me when I sat on the couch.

"You should see a doctor about that."

He chuckled, but we both knew damned well that it wasn't him he'd been talking about. "Yeah. OK. Deny all you want, but I see the way you look at her."

"You see nothing. You're probably drunk when you think you see anything worth noting."

"Nope. Sober as can be and you still look like you want to devour the poor woman. Now she's here for a week. I don't think you'll last three days."

"You think I'm just going to pounce on her?"

He faked an offended look. "Of course not. It'd be consensual, but given how she looks at you, I don't think you'd have to work very hard for it."

"Fuck off." That was my go-to response most of the time and it took a lot of control not to put more force behind the words.

I didn't like him talking about Charlotte that way. It didn't sit well with me at all.

For the next hour, I sat right there on the couch tinkering with my guitar. That was what I called it when I was playing but not playing anything specific. Or if I was working out a song. Jamison went to bed not long after I'd told him to fuck off so I could enjoy being alone.

Until I wasn't alone anymore.

"Sorry," Charlotte said as she pulled at the hem of her tank top. Her feet were also sliding against one another like she was uncomfortable. "I didn't realize anyone was still awake."

"There's always someone awake on this bus." Which was mostly true if you counted the driver. "Couldn't sleep?"

She shook her head quickly. "It's been a weird day."

I patted the other side of the couch so she'd sit down. If she was going to be here, I wanted her to be comfortable and there'd be plenty of space between us. Charlotte hurried over then sat on the couch with her legs crossed and her feet under her.

"Thanks for earlier," she said as she tucked a lock of blonde hair behind her ear. The color was so flattering that I assumed it was her natural one.

"Earlier?"

"Getting me outside for some air. I needed it."

"Yeah, you looked like you were going to pass out." I stopped strumming the guitar to take a drink of the water that was sitting beside me. "Is that how it always is when you see blood?"

After swallowing hard, Charlotte nodded. "I don't like blood."

"You said that." My eyes met hers. "Is there a reason for that?"

Since it'd happened and I'd seen her reaction to the blood, which had been such a small amount, I worried that it was because of something that had happened to her. She looked fine. I didn't see any scars, but I also hadn't seen *all* of her.

That was when she turned her arm over and I saw a scar. Trying not to react, I set my guitar aside then leaned in for a closer look. The thin, light line ran down the inside of her arm, like it'd happened a long time ago and I prayed that the next words out of her mouth weren't that she'd done this to herself.

I didn't know how I would react to that.

This sweet, beautiful woman who had my cock half hard just by being in the room couldn't have done something to herself. I wouldn't accept it.

"It's because of the day I got this," she said. Our gazes locked and it was like I could feel it. She was looking at me, but she might as well have been touching me. For me, it was the same thing.

"What happened?"

Charlotte took in a deep breath and blew it out slowly. "I never tell anyone about this."

"You don't have to."

"But I want to tell you," she said softly. I ran a hand through my hair to make her think I was chill about it, but every nerve in my body was on alert. I was ready to tear the world apart depending on what she said. "It's from a car accident." The muscles in my body relaxed. "When I was fourteen, I was in the car with my grandpa, my mom's dad, and a semi driver had fallen asleep. It was bad and my grandpa was killed—but not instantly."

My stomach tightened, thinking about her in that car and my heart fucking broke for her. "I'm sorry, Charlotte."

She took another breath and her eyes began to water, which made me regret asking anything in the first place.

"Thank you. I was stuck in that car with him while he slowly died and then with his body until they could get me out. It was two hours they said before they got me out. I'd gotten cut on the flying glass and was holding on so tightly to stop the bleeding that I couldn't do anything for my grandpa."

That fucking sucked. "Do you think you could have done anything anyway?"

She shook her head sadly. "He was going to die

either way, but he kept asking for my grandma and asking if I was OK until he couldn't talk anymore." I moved closer before reaching out to her, cradling the arm she'd been holding in my hand, and stroked her scar with my thumb. "My grandma had died when I was little. I don't have a lot of memories of her, but she was all he wanted when he was dying. It took years of therapy for me to get through it, but I did." She whispered, "I just don't usually like to talk about it."

"You don't have to," I said quietly. "But that's why you don't like blood?"

She nodded. "There was..." She shuddered. "So much of it between his and mine. I just..." She swallowed hard. "I don't like the sight of it."

I'd do anything in my power to make sure she never saw another drop of it again.

Who was I kidding? She was on this bus for mere days. I didn't control the world and she wasn't mine to protect. Not to mention, the memories of my own that kept popping into my head right then, but it wasn't the fucking same.

For some reason, I hadn't let go of her arm and I honestly didn't want to. She wasn't pulling away, either so when the urge hit me, I did nothing to try to stop it.

Keeping the one hand on her arm, my thumb still stroking that scar, I took the other and cupped her face. Our eyes met and everything else in the world fell away. It'd been a long fucking time since someone had looked at me with that kind of tenderness and I hadn't realized that I'd missed it.

Slowly, I brought her forward as I moved in. When our lips touched, my world changed. Charlotte didn't pull back. Quite the opposite. She rested a hand on my chest as she leaned into the kiss. She parted her sweet lips so that I could stroke her tongue with mine, then she pushed forward even more, climbing onto my lap without breaking our connection.

I grasped her hips while she cupped my face in her hands. This... This right here was different than any kiss I'd ever experienced. These days, a kiss was meant to lead to something else. It was the beginning of my pleasurable end and while I wanted inside of Charlotte more than I'd ever wanted anything in my life, I already knew that this wasn't leading there. I wouldn't let it. She deserved more than a quick fuck on a tour bus. I'd never be able to look at her as a one-night stand, so I wouldn't make her one.

Her hips swayed, causing her to grind into my

erection, which was no longer half-hard. It was fucking *granite* in my jeans. Having her on top of me this way was making it incredibly difficult to remind myself not to let this go too far.

When I brought the kiss to an end, Charlotte looked at me with confusion before realization hit her. What she realized, I wasn't sure until she skittered off my lap.

"I'm so sorry," she said, pacing the little area in front of me. She slapped her hand over her face. "I can't believe I just did that."

"Did what?"

She stopped and let her hands fall to her sides, slapping the exposed skin on her legs. "I just climbed you like a tree. How embarrassing."

A low chuckle rumbled in my chest as I stood in front of her. "That is not embarrassing."

"Yes, it is. I tell you my sad story and then climb into your lap like a needy puppy." Her deep-blue eyes finally met mine. "I'm so sorry. It won't happen again. Kenzie will be so sad if you kick us off the bus in the morning. This is like a dream come true to her."

I settled my hands on her shoulders, trying to ignore how smooth her skin was beneath my fingers.

"Charlotte." Once I knew she was paying attention, I continued. "*I* kissed *you*. You didn't do anything."

"But—" she started. My thumbs swiping gently over her cheeks cut her off. She closed her eyes, like she wanted to savor the feeling, and I let her, waiting until she opened her eyes again.

"I stopped for reasons of my own. You did nothing wrong."

"But—"

Again, I stopped her. "Now I'm going to go to bed before I regret my decision even more than I already do."

She nodded slowly, but with the way her hungry eyes were on me, I needed to get away before I threw good manners out the window.

When I looked back before climbing into my bunk, I saw she hadn't moved. "And it'd be a real tragedy if that never happened again."

Her mouth opened slightly, but I jumped into my bunk before she had a chance to respond.

It took a long fucking time for my dick to soften enough that I could fall asleep.

8

CHARLOTTE

I lay awake in the bunk next to Kenzie for a long time obsessing over that kiss and what it might've led to. My sex life was limited, but not non-existent. I wasn't a virgin, but it'd been a while and I didn't have that many people in my history, mostly because I can't do a damn thing without a babysitter.

And while I hadn't had sex with London, that kiss was so good, I may as well have. It was better than any kiss I'd experienced because the man *knew* how to kiss. Which probably meant he knew how to do other things as well. But of course, he would. He was a damn rock star.

Sleep finally found me, but I knew it was late. Or

early, depending on how you looked at it. The distinct sound of the brakes from the bus was the last thing I heard before dozing off.

When I woke hours later, I was alone in the bunk, so I took the opportunity to stretch out. There were enough bunks for her and me to have our own, but we'd felt better sharing. After all, everyone was new to us and when we'd made that decision, it'd felt right.

There was a low murmur coming from the main space, but they were feminine voices, which meant either the guys were out there and not talking or they weren't out there.

Still, I lay there for a while, hoping to wait until London had left. They had radio spots to do this morning and if I was lucky, I'd miss seeing him first thing. The worry that everyone would know we'd kissed by the way I looked at him was real.

The shade slid back. "Wake up, sleepyhead." Kenzie's face hovered over mine, giving me a heart attack.

"Why do you do that?"

She snickered. "You need to get up."

"Yes, but I don't need to wake up to your face inches from mine."

"I want you to feel loved."

While shaking my head at her, I did a full body stretch. However long I'd slept, it hadn't been long enough. As I pushed myself up to climb out, I paused. "Who's out there?"

"Just Lilah and Becca, but they're getting ready to go to work."

Well, that was a relief. If everyone else was gone, then I was safe to get out looking like I'd just climbed out of bed.

"Good morning," Lilah and Becca sang at the same time in much-too-cheerful voices.

I reached into the fridge for a bottle of water and drained a good part of it before saying it back.

"Looks like you were tired." Lilah smirked and fear ran through me. Did she know something? She couldn't. London and I had been alone last night.

"I had a hard time falling asleep."

"That happened to me when I first started on the bus," Becca told me. "It passes pretty quickly, but it sucked."

"Listen, Becca and I have to go get things ready for tonight, but want to have dinner? Just the four of us?" Lilah grabbed a bag from the couch then turned to us.

"Sounds good to me," I told her. Kenzie agreed.

Once those two had left, Kenzie turned to me. "Lilah said we can shower in the venue. The guys aren't here because of their interviews or whatever, so now would be a good time. Then do you want to grab a bagel and go exploring? I've never been to Cincinnati."

"That all sounds great, but I'm getting coffee with my bagel."

"Of course."

The bus had a shower, but we'd been told not to use it. The pressure sucked and it took up the water supply that would be better spent on flushing the toilet. Apparently, there was someone who emptied the septic tank or whatever the bus had on it. I'd asked because I was always curious about the oddest things.

That left showering to the venue or hotel when they stayed at one and with the band gone, it was the perfect chance.

Kenzie and I grabbed our bags and the hair stuff that Lilah had left out for us and headed inside. We showered together, but it wasn't like we were standing right next to each other and since we shared an apartment, we'd seen each other naked before.

We both pulled our hair into buns because that

was easy. Though mine would be a kinky mess later, I didn't care at the moment. Then we were dressed, we'd dropped our stuff off back, at the bus and we were on our own.

The closest coffee shop was the first stop, though instead of a bagel, I got a donut that looked so good. Kenzie did the same.

Once we were done, she asked, "So what should we do?"

"I don't know." I shrugged.

"I think there's a river walk not too far away." She looked down at her phone and scrolled. "We could spend some time just walking and seeing whatever from there, then do some shopping. It depends on how active you want to be."

"Not active. In fact, if I could go back to bed, that would be sweet."

She snorted. "No way. I know you've been everywhere, but I'm not missing this opportunity."

I nudged her with my hip. "I've been everywhere, but I've seen nothing. You know this. Let's do the walk and if there's time, shopping. If not, that's cool too. We have to meet the girls for dinner, then we're going to the concert tonight."

"True. It's just nice to be out."

"Exactly."

"Though I can't believe you're giving up shopping."

The two of us giggled, but I decided to be real. "You know damn well that I only shop as much as I do to stick the credit card bill to my dad. I can't let him see the charges right now."

"Which never fazes him."

We'd started walking in the direction of the riverfront walk and it hadn't taken long. Now we were slowly strolling, with our coffees in hand, down the riverfront.

"It never fazes him," I told her, "because I never buy enough for him to notice. Maybe I should start with crazy expensive cars."

"Yeah, but then he'd be pissed at you for being flashy."

"That's true and honestly, I don't even want his money. I'd like to be too big of a problem that he decides to cut me loose."

"That reminds me." She snapped her finger. "Your brother messaged after I was in bed last night so I didn't see it until this morning. He's glad you're alive and thought you'd like to know that your parents are going crazy trying to find you."

"Good."

She nodded in agreement. "But you know that means the snap when you get back is going to be bigger than ever."

"I can handle it."

"He also said to have fun and let him know if you need anything." She slid her phone back into her pocket. "I love AJ."

"Me too." AJ was really Andrew Joshua the Seventeenth or something crazy. He preferred "AJ," so my parents called him "Andrew."

My brother would have my back no matter what. Despite our upbringing and family, we'd formed a relationship that wouldn't be broken.

The day was bright and warm with a small breeze coming off the water. It was so beautiful that when we found a bench, we took a seat. There was no hurry to get back to the venue. After all, we were guests and guests sometimes started to get annoying. The band was busy. The girls were busy. Kenzie and I were the only ones without a purpose and we didn't want to be in the way.

"Have you thought about what you want to do since you don't want to do politics like your dad?" she asked as we sipped on our coffees.

"Not really."

"I call bullshit, Charlotte. There has to be something that you've dreamed of."

She knew me too well to lie again. "I honestly am not totally sure and we still have a year of school left."

"I know. I know. What about after?"

I took a deep breath as I prepared to tell my best friend something that I hadn't told anyone. Not because it was a deep, dark secret, but because telling someone meant that someone else knew. It didn't make a lot of sense, but in my house, you always kept things pretty close to the vest, as they say. If my father found out one of us was stepping off the path he'd chosen without his permission, he would've found a way to shut it down. AJ had only gotten away with med school because my father had found it acceptable. Who wouldn't vote for a doctor in the future?

"You know my dad's dream is to have a political dynasty."

"I do." She nodded. "His way of legitimizing the family because of your dark beginnings." She said it as if it were salacious and I couldn't help but laugh.

Well, it *was* kind of salacious, I suppose.

"Right, so if he ever found out before I did something else, he'd make sure it didn't happen. You know that."

"I'm not going to tell anyone. You know this," she said. I did, but sometimes, I needed the reassurance.

"I've often thought that I'd love to open an animal rescue."

"Aww."

"Right? You know I love animals and there's so much need. With my trust fund, which my father will no longer have control of once I graduate, I could get off to a great start and then I could find donors and all of that to just keep growing so we'd never have to turn any animal away."

"I love that idea." She paused because if I knew Kenzie, which I did, she didn't want to stay the hard parts out loud in case I took it as her dashing my dreams. Which I got enough of from my family.

"What?"

She sighed and turned to me. "It's so much work."

"I know. I'm not afraid of work and I'll hire people, beg for volunteers."

"It could be really sad. You might not want to put any animals down, but they could still come in sick or injured. They could die."

I swallowed hard. That wasn't the part I was

looking forward to, yet it was true. "I know. But I think that they all deserve love, especially toward the end."

"Well, I really love this idea for you. You somehow have such a big heart and I know you'd be awesome at it."

"Thank you."

One thing I could count on was Kenzie always having faith in me and saying it out loud. Without her, I didn't know where I'd be.

The two of us spent hours walking around and taking pictures of things we found interesting and selfies that I always reminded her she couldn't post until we were home. She'd roll her eyes each time because she knew. I knew she knew, but I had to say it.

It'd be so relaxing to not have to worry about that stuff in another year. Once I'm done with school, the things about my life that they control will go away. That doesn't mean they won't try but I will be much freer.

As we slowly walked back toward the venue— thank you, GPS—I knew I had to tell her about what had happened last night, but again, I didn't want to make it real. Scratch that. I knew it was real. I could still feel his lips on me, but I didn't want to share it because it was just for London and me.

But Kenzie was my best friend and she would've told me if she'd been in my shoes.

"I kissed London last night," I said, as if I were telling her the sky was blue.

She stopped in her tracks and said, much too loudly, "*What*?"

I turned back to her. "I kissed London last night."

"I heard you." She reached out and grabbed my wrists. "Why am I *just* hearing about this? Why were we talking about things that don't matter like the future when we could've been talking about this? Plus, I fucking told you so."

I snickered at her rambling. "I don't know why I didn't wake you up last night when I came back to bed to tell you that we'd kissed. That was my bad."

"Yes. It was," she said seriously. "Tell me everything and I swear to the universe that you'd better not leave a single detail out.

So I did. I told her everything that had happened, including me climbing him like a tree. A desperate tree. And the fact that I would've had sex with him right there, which wasn't like me at all. It was still true, though.

"I can't believe you kissed a rock star." She held her hands out and yelled at the city, "A rock star!"

"Not everyone needs to know about it." I turned and started walking again.

"I beg to disagree. Was it good?"

I gave her an *are you kidding me* look with scrunched-up brows and pursed lips. "What do you think?"

"I think he probably has a lot of experience, so it should've been amazing."

"It was a great kiss." That was all I was going to give her on that.

"What does it mean? Are you going to have sex with him? Marry him? Ohmygod, your father would lose his mind."

"I don't know what it means, but I am pretty sure it doesn't mean I'm marrying him, though my father losing his shit does have some appeal." I let that image take over for a few seconds before I continued. "I told him about the accident."

"You did?" Her voice was softer now. I nodded. "You don't tell people about that."

"I know, but he asked about me freaking out at Jamison's blood and it... felt right, I guess."

She cocked her head to the side. "Will you take his name or hyphenate? Will you be Charlotte Kerr or Charlotte Andersen-Kerr? I wouldn't hyphenate because why be connected to your family?"

Giggling and shaking my head was all I could do. Kenzie was ridiculous sometimes, but she was my best friend and that was what mattered.

Though now that I'd told her about the kiss, it was all that I could think about. That and wondering if it was going to happen again.

F uck my life.

I'd done everything there was to do, or at least everything I was interested in doing, yet right now I was sitting in a radio booth, answering questions that everyone had heard a hundred times with a fucking hard-on thinking about Charlotte on my lap last night.

At least with four other band members, I could let them take the lead. However, that meant I could let my imagination run wild and that didn't help the big issue I had going south of the border.

Her skin had been soft, her mouth so fucking sweet. Like ripe strawberries in the middle of summer.

I'd better never say that out loud because I'd never hear the end of it.

We finished up the radio spot on the local station then did a few of those intro recordings that could be used at all the stations owned by the same company. For some reason, that took for fucking ever and we couldn't get in sync.

It shouldn't have been hard for all of us to say, "*Hi. We're Forever 18 and you're listing to {insert radio station here}.*" Though we had a list of a bunch to run down and this was getting frustrating.

Finally, we were done and headed to soundcheck.

I was fucking starving but knew we wouldn't have a chance to eat until after.

We might've been shit at recording radio spots, but we were all together on soundcheck, which meant it only took about twenty minutes.

Now we could eat.

The five of us were walking down the hallway when Jamison said, "If I don't eat soon, I'm going to start eating one of you and it won't be in the fun way."

"Why wouldn't you find a restaurant instead?" Thatcher countered.

"That's what I'm saying. Feed me or become a

cannibalistic feast." He glanced around. "Hang on. Where are the women? Do we have to wait for them because if we do, I swear to—"

"No." Grayson cut him off. "Lilah sent me a text to let me know she's out to dinner with Becca, Kenzie, and Charlotte. We're good."

My chest tightened when he'd mentioned her name and I knew this was stupid. I'd just met the woman. She didn't mean anything to me, yet for some reason, she kind of did. I couldn't figure out why. I'd kissed more women than I could count and had only thought about one after.

Until Charlotte.

"Where are we going?" I asked to get my mind on something else.

"I don't fucking care," Jamison countered. "Anywhere that has food. What's the closest place?"

The closest restaurant was a chain, but luckily for us, it wasn't busy and they could seat us right away. Before the waitress walked away, he begged her to bring three appetizers ASAP. She gave him a smile and said she'd do it just for him.

That was how Jamison got everything he wanted.

We talked about the show tonight and some other things going on with the band until our food came. Even though the appetizers had held Jamison off, he dove into his burger as if he hadn't eaten in a week. We'd all ordered burgers because it was easy. It was good, but it couldn't compare to this burger place just north of us back home.

"How long are the women staying?" Jamison asked through his mouthful of food.

"Which ones?" Thatcher countered.

Grayson shook his head. "You know damn well that Lilah and Becca are here for the entire tour. How would you get dressed without them?"

Jamison nodded as he finished chewing and somehow, maybe a feeling in the air, I knew he was going to say something Grayson wasn't going to like. "I have to say that I don't hate the fact that your woman puts her hands on me every once in a while. Or that she's seen me almost naked."

Fucking Jamison. I had to give it to Grayson. He didn't leap over the table and choke the man. We both knew that if he let Jamison know it bothered him, he'd double his efforts.

"Yeah. After seeing you in your underwear, she told me how unimpressed she was," he countered. "Asked if women slept with you because they feel bad for what you're... lacking."

Jamison held up a middle finger while the rest of us roared. Once we calmed down, Lennox told him,

"If you're talking about Charlotte and Kenzie, just the week, right? Just until we're back in Detroit."

Grayson told him he was right, but the thought of Charlotte heading back to Ann Arbor made my skin feel tight. This was ridiculous. I barely knew her.

The concert went off without a hitch. We played our best and the crowd loved every minute of it. So did we.

Me, though, I couldn't keep my eyes off Charlotte as she danced and sang with Kenzie out there living her best life. Her mouth forming the words I'd written was especially sweet, even if she didn't know all of them. We all wrote songs, so she was mouthing all of our words, but when I knew they were mine, it was different.

Playing guitar and adding a little backup vocals meant I had a lot of time to watch her, though she only caught me doing so once.

Once we were done, I hopped into the shower for the quickest one of my life. It was unusual that I was alone in the shower and I entertained the idea of relieving some of the pressure that had been building since Charlotte last night but thought better of it. This was supposed to be quick. I could do that anytime.

When I stepped out of the dressing room, the other guys had come into the shower halfway through mine with the same idea that I'd had. Quick shower. We had a massive meet and greet tonight. But I was done first and in the packed hallway.

That was when I saw Charlotte trying to break free of the crowd and my stomach tightened. I didn't like seeing her in that mass of people.

I pushed through until I was beside her and placed my hand on her lower back to lead her away from the commotion. It wasn't like it was wall to wall people, but it was crowded.

Sean had put this together tonight, meeting a ton of people we'd been putting off for a while, because we had such a short trip to Chicago. That meant we could leave late and still be fine.

Once I got Charlotte away from the people, I ripped open the door closest to us. I had no idea what the room was, but I knew that it was probably empty and that was all I cared about. Then it was the two of us in this small room. I flipped the lights on.

It looked like the place was used for storage.

She sucked her bottom lip into her mouth then let it out quickly. "Thank you for that. I thought it would never end."

"Sometimes you have to be a little forceful."

She took in a breath and intertwined her fingers. This was the first time I really noticed what she was wearing. A pair of shorts that were short enough to make her legs look long, but not so short anyone else would've been able to see her ass cheeks. I called that fucking perfection. She'd paired it with a Forever 18 T-shirt that looked nice and worn. Meaning she'd been wearing it for a while or it was Kenzie's given that she was the bigger fan of ours. With her blonde hair hanging in waves over her shoulder, she looked so fucking innocent.

A not-so-gentle reminder that I shouldn't corrupt her.

"Oh, no." Her eyes widened. "Kenzie."

"She's fine," I told her. "She was standing in the back scrolling on her phone like she was waiting it out. She'll be fine."

She nodded then the two of us stood there watching each other. Until Charlotte swallowed hard and opened her mouth.

"You kissed me last night."

I chuckled. "I was there."

"Now you have me in this room alone. No one knows we're in here," she whispered. My fucking dick hardened. "Are you going to kiss me again?"

"I shouldn't," I said right away. "I fucking want to, but I shouldn't."

Charlotte took a step closer to me. "But I want you to."

There was no stopping me, then. She'd said she wanted it and I wasn't about to deny her. I pushed my hand into her hair while cupping her jaw. Her hair was smoother than her skin and felt like feathers over my fingers. Then I lowered my mouth to hers.

So fucking sweet.

Her hands settled on biceps like she was trying to reach higher, but she was so fucking small next to me that there was nowhere else for her to go. My other hand settled on her hip, but my fingers poked in under her shirt.

She didn't stop me.

The door to the room opened as my tongue slid against her. I took the hand in her hair and pushed the door shut with a slam. I didn't break that kiss, but I did hear someone on the other side say something about almost taking off their fucking fingers. I hadn't hit anything so it was just a close call but I didn't give a shit.

No one was coming in here as long as Charlotte was letting me kiss her.

I walked her back to the door so that no one else would be able to get it open a crack. Resting one hand against the wall, I let the other slide up Charlotte's back to pull her toward me. There wasn't much room between us or her and the door.

We kissed like high schoolers saying goodnight after the dance. I wanted to do so much more and if this had been another woman who was willing, I would have. But not Charlotte. I wasn't going to fuck her in a closet against the door before going to do a meet and greet.

Wasn't going to happen.

Reluctantly, I had to pull away.

Her fingers immediately brushed against her bottom lip.

"I have to go," I told her quietly while giving her no space.

"Right." She looked up at me with those big, blue eyes. "People are waiting."

I nodded slowly but still didn't move. The last thing I wanted to do right then was leave her, but it was what I needed to do. Even if there hadn't been people waiting on me.

"I'll... see you later," I told her. A smile played at her lips as she ducked under my arm and turned the doorknob. Charlotte walked out of this tiny room as if she didn't care who saw her leave or what they might've assumed once I'd left too.

I sure as fuck didn't care what people thought about me, but I did care what they thought about her.

Still, I left the room too and found the guys so we could get this night over with.

It was a steady stream of names and handshakes or hugs for the fans. So many pictures that I worried my mouth was going to freeze in the smiling position. Or that I'd never smile again after this.

Once we were done, everyone scattered to do their own thing. We still had time before we were going to pull out.

Grayson headed out of the arena, I assumed to the bus, where Lilah would've been waiting for him, and I followed. There wasn't anything else I wanted to do, though seeing Charlotte was going to be hard because whenever she was near me, I wanted my hands on her.

"What's going on with you and Charlotte?" Grayson asked once we'd stepped out into the night. I stiffened. It was cooler outside than it had been before the concert and when he stopped, I did too. Apparently, this wasn't a conversation he wanted to have on the bus.

"Nothing. What do you mean?"

"I saw you go into that room with her." He held a finger up. "Scratch that. I saw you come out of that room with her. I can only imagine what happened in there."

I stepped closer. "You shouldn't be imagining shit. Nothing happened."

"Right."

"She was stuck in the crowd of people. I got her out. That's it."

Grayson contemplated me for a moment before saying, "You know it's OK to care about someone, right? You don't have to keep punishing yourself."

My jaw tightened. "I'm not."

"You are. And I figured one day, you'd meet someone who made you stop. Is Charlotte that person?"

"I don't know what you're talking about." I turned to head toward the bus.

"Are you telling me nothing happened between you two?" he called out, making me stop and turn back. It was only seconds before Grayson was right in front of me again.

"We kissed. Nothing more."

His eyebrows shot up. "You kissed?"

"Twice. But that's it. I didn't realize you're the puritan police."

He snorted. "I'm not. But the fact that you only kissed her when you could've fucked her says something."

"All it says is that I didn't have the time."

"The fuck it does." Grayson took a deep breath and folded his hands over his chest. "You are allowed to be happy, London. What happened with Holly wasn't your fault."

"Of course it wasn't. I didn't give her epilepsy."

"Then what's your fucking problem? You've met a woman you like—don't try to tell me that you don't —so let yourself be happy."

I shook my head because he didn't get it.

Grayson fucked around like the rest of us, but he'd also had a steady stream of girlfriends. Now he had Lilah, but they were still happy. Nothing stood in their way. He had no idea how much fucking pain came with that level of love. It was too high of a price to pay.

"Can't you go bury yourself in your woman and leave me alone?"

"I can." He smiled widely. "And I will. But not without you hearing me first." He stepped closer. "I know you better than anyone, London. I was there when Holly died and saw how much that hurt you. That doesn't mean you should ignore what's right in front of you. I've never seen a woman more made for you than Charlotte."

"You don't even know her."

"I know enough."

Finally, he walked away, leaving me alone. Only now, the last place I wanted to go was that damn bus. A world of heartache awaited me there no matter what I chose. I fucking yearned for Charlotte and not letting myself have her would be something I thought about probably for the rest of my life. Letting her in and something happening would be a whole world worse.

Somehow, though, no matter how rational I thought I was being, I couldn't fucking stay away.

10

CHARLOTTE

"That was a great show," Kenzie said as we changed our clothes on the bus.

We thought it best to do that before everyone got here. Sure, we could still do it in our bunk or even the bathroom or back room—it was just a little more difficult. Plus, I wanted to get out of those sweaty clothes.

The memory of London's lips on mine and the carnal need that had filled me at that moment lingered in my mind. I'd never felt that kind of need before and if I were being honest, it hadn't gone away. Every touch had heightened it.

"It was," I said, in response to Kenzie's comment about the show.

"I feel like London put a little extra something into his performance." She glanced at me with a knowing look, but I wasn't sure what she thought she knew. "Like maybe he wanted to be extra good for someone."

"I doubt that." I crumpled up my clothes and stuffed them back in the bag.

"What's with the tone?"

"No tone."

Kenzie put her hands on her hips and raised her eyebrows. She was doing the waiting thing. Waiting for me to spill whatever I was feeling.

There was no use waiting her out, so I sighed.

"He kissed me after the show."

"Again?" Her entire body exploded with excitement. "I need the details."

"You need to quiet down." The buses were definitely not soundproof.

"OK. OK." Kenzie took my hands and led me to the couch, basically forcing me to sit, though I almost wanted to pace. There was so much energy inside me that I needed to get out. Maybe a talk would do that. "Tell me everything."

So I did. I told her about him finding me in the crowd after I'd lost her. She apologized for not keeping up and instead hanging back until it cleared. I didn't care about that. We were both big girls and could take care of ourselves.

I gave her the details that she was thirsting for, but all it did was leave me kind of deflated.

"He definitely likes kissing you."

"*Only* kissing me." As soon as the words were out of my mouth, I wished I hadn't said them.

Kenzie put her hands against her chest like I'd just surprised her. "Wait. You want more? My little girl now wants the random hookup with a rock star?"

This was why I wished I hadn't said it. "It's not that, Kenzie. It's..." I groaned and fell back onto the couch to stare at the ceiling. "It's not a random hookup that I'm after, though at this point, I'm pretty needy, so I think I'd take it." Based on the sound of her giggle, I knew she was covering her mouth in a failed attempt to muffle herself. "It's... I like him. He's nice to me, which you know is a departure from my usual life. AJ is nice to me, of course, but even the men I've dated... they've only been as nice as they have to be to please my father." I pushed myself up to look at her. "And London doesn't even know who my father *is*, let alone want to please him."

"I get it, Charlotte. You don't think Daddy issues are making you cling to London, do you?"

I scowled at her. "I don't have Daddy issues. I have *an* issue with my father and I'm not clinging to London Kerr."

She held her hands up. "I was just asking."

Before we could continue our talk, Lilah and Becca climbed onto the bus. All talk of London was strictly forbidden now and Kenzie knew it. Those conversations were just for us.

The four of us spent our time laughing and talking. We told stories about different things, though I was careful not to give away anything about my family. Usually once I did, everything changed and this friendship with those two was so easy that I didn't want it to change.

It was a long time before the guys returned. Lilah had said tonight was going to be late because Grayson had told her that Sean was using tonight as a catchup. There were people they needed to meet. People with whom they'd be working in the future and just favors that Sean owed people for favors he'd gotten for the band. I didn't understand it all, but I didn't need to.

I was mid-yawn when London climbed onto the bus last. His eyes found me immediately and now my skin was warm again, even though I was wearing shorts and a tank top, just like last night. Grayson snorted and when I glanced at him, I realized he'd been watching London.

Damn it. Way for him to ruin my moment.

London scowled at Grayson before heading down the hallway. As he passed me, his fingers brushed my arm low enough that no one else should've been able to see it.

Grayson saw it and snorted again then had a big grin on his face when I looked at him.

I shook my head and announced, "I'm going to bed."

"Want me to come?" Kenzie asked and I knew it was in case I needed to talk some more.

"I'm good. I'll just cuddle your pillow if I get lonely."

The guys chuckled and I realized that it might've been a little weird that she and I were still sharing a bunk now that we knew everyone a little bit and clearly weren't worried that we weren't safe.

London was standing near me when I stood up. He took up most of the hallway with one hand on the wall and the other on the counter when our eyes locked. There was so much exchanged in that look that it had me fighting a shiver. Everything that look promised, I wanted.

"Did you hear that, London?" Grayson asked. "Charlotte says she might get lonely."

London dropped his hand from the wall and moved aside so that I could get by him. "Fuck off." He said it to Grayson but was watching me as I moved past.

Once I got into the bunk and settled in, I could only hear the low murmur of what was happening out there. It made me wish that I'd stayed out there, but I didn't think I could be so close to London without giving away everything I was feeling.

I was still awake when Kenzie climbed over me. For whatever reason, she was happier sleeping on the inside, which meant she had to go over me to get there. She did that once in my bed at the apartment when she'd come home drunk. Even though she could've just gone around the other side of the bed. Here, she didn't have a choice.

Her steady breathing was almost instant and since I had no idea what time it was, I figured she was just tired. I wished I was. Between my sexual frustration and the idea of running an animal shelter that, now that I'd spoken about it out loud was becoming an obsession, I couldn't get to sleep. I'd been yawning earlier but now was wide awake. And getting a headache from lying here.

Quietly, I slipped out the bunk and tiptoed to the back room, where our bags were, so I could get my laptop. I'd brought it with me because I'd faked going to an exam and Donovan would've thought it weird that I didn't have my backpack. Then I wasn't going to leave it in the car when we'd left it.

Now, I was going to use it to tire me out.

I settled in at the table and began my research. I wanted to run an animal shelter and it was time to figure out if that was even possible. I'd get no financial help from my parents and honestly, I liked it better that way. I'd have my trust fund because my dad couldn't keep that from me once I graduated from college.

That was the deal. I'd get it upon graduation or my father could've chosen to allow me access early. Thanks, Grandpa.

I was there reading away when London dropped onto the seat across from me. Glancing up, I was surprised to see him, even though I'd known it was him.

"Hi," I said, then I waited for him.

"I heard you get up a while ago and was waiting for you to get back into your bunk. You didn't."

"I couldn't sleep."

He leaned his elbows on the table and folded his hand just below his face. "Something wrong?"

I slowly shook my head. "Thinking about things."

"Things?"

"Two things." I didn't want him to think that he was the only thing keeping me up, but somewhere along the way, I'd decided that I wouldn't hide what I was feeling for him. The attraction. All of it. Even if I was just realizing that decision had been made.

He took a breath then sat back. "What are you thinking about?"

There was a moment as I decided which thing to start with, but the longer it lasted, the more I wanted to blurt out my sexual need to him. Instead, I decided to play it safe.

"What I want to do after graduation."

"And what does Charlotte Andersen want to do after graduation?"

"I've always wanted to run an animal shelter. I know it sounds stupid, but—"

"It doesn't sound stupid at all, Charlotte." He took a drink from the water bottle on the table. It didn't seem to matter that it was mine. I didn't care, but there was a level of intimacy that went along with that. "That's a big-hearted thing to do."

"I guess I've got a big heart, then. So I finally admitted it to Kenzie yesterday and now I'm researching what I need to do to open it. I have a year until graduation and things will move quickly right after. I want to be ready."

"What do you mean things will move quickly?"

Yeah. I'd said that and now I was going to have to walk a thin line of explaining it to him without letting him know who my father was. "My parents insisted that I major in Political Science. They have political aspirations for me, but I'm not about that life. My brother is in med school, so he's doing his passion and that was OK with them." Our eyes locked. "Because who doesn't want a doctor in the family? Not to mention, in their eyes him being a doctor helps any future political aspirations. He has none but our father doesn't take no easily."

"I assume no one."

"Anyway, I inherited some money from my grandpa." His eyes softened at the mention of my grandpa because I'd already told him about the accident. "I want to use that to get started and then I'll have to fundraise and maybe get some donors to keep it open. It'll be hard, but I think I'll love it."

Somewhere between confessing my deep, dark wish for my life to Kenzie and this moment at the table, I'd decided to do it. It was both scary and exciting at the same time.

"I'll donate," he said right away. "I'm sure the band will too. We're always looking for something charitable to be involved in and we all love animals."

"You don't have to—"

"It's done, Charlotte. You tell me what you need and if we can make it happen, we will. Plus..." He got this cheesy grin on his face. "We're rock stars. We know other rock stars. I'd bet we could get you everything. No problem."

Emotion swelled in my chest. "Thank you." And I wouldn't let him go back on that promise. Not that I thought he would.

"What's the other thing?"

At first I was confused. Until I remembered that I'd told him there were two things keeping me up. "I'd rather not say," I said softly. He narrowed his eyes on me. "It's kind of embarrassing to admit."

He leaned over the table and since he was so freaking tall, he was so close. "Charlotte. You shouldn't be embarrassed about anything around me."

I swallowed hard. That was easy for *him* to say. "You," I told him, which had him pulling back and confused.

"Me?"

I nodded but hadn't blinked. "You're keeping me up."

"How? I was in my bunk. Quiet as a mouse."

Taking in a deep breath to steady my nerves, I blew it out slowly and hoped that he wouldn't see that I was shaky. "You kissed me earlier."

His jaw clenched as he ran a hand through his brown hair, the apology in his hazel eyes before he said it.

"Don't apologize," I told him before he could. "It was a good kiss. But..." Time to put it on the table. "It's been a while since I've..." Suddenly, my mouth was completely dry, so I snatched the bottle of water from his side of the table and drank the rest of it.

Before I could finish, he did. "Had sex?" he said. I nodded and squirmed in my seat. This was more uncomfortable than I'd expected. "It was a kiss."

"You can't be that clueless," I told him. "It was a really good kiss."

He thought about that, or that was what I assumed he was thinking about, then one corner of his mouth lifted. "So the kiss turned you on." He leaned over the table again. "The kiss got you wet."

I groaned and slapped a hand over my face. If I could've burrowed down into the seat, I would have.

"Yes. OK? It's been a while since I've had sex, so your kiss had me wanting to get naked in the damn closet."

He chuckled, but somehow, I knew it was at the last part and not the first.

His face grew more serious. "I don't do the girl-friend thing, Charlotte."

A fluttering butterfly took flight in my chest. "I'm not asking you to."

"With you, I just don't see how it can be avoided."

"I'm leaving in a few days, London. I think it can be avoided pretty easily." But the way he said it might not be something he can resist had my thoughts going all over the place. My stomach had the same feeling as if I was on a boat. This gorgeous man who doesn't do girlfriends actually thought I might've been the one to change that.

"So you want a hookup."

No. That wasn't what I wanted because I had a decent understanding that if I were to have sex with London and then he was out of my life, I'd miss him forever. That was a chance I'd have to take if it was to happen.

"That's not what I'm saying." I took a breath as this got easier the further we went. "It's not that I want to hook up with you. Hit it and quit. Whatever.

It's that you kissed me earlier and now I can't sleep. That's all I was saying."

He wet the bottom lip with his tongue as he nodded slowly. Maybe he did understand. I didn't know, but I was ready for this embarrassment to be over.

"I can help you with that," he finally said, but when I didn't understand, he continued. "I can't help you with not sleeping. But I need you to understand that I don't do the girlfriend thing. Haven't in a really long time and don't intend to ever again."

"You told me that already." Yet him saying it again had me wanting to ask why it was he didn't have girlfriends, but if I did that right now, it'd be over.

"Yeah, but I need you to know it."

"I do, London. Look. I'm not asking you to do anything. I just answered your question. We can let it die now."

He pushed up from the seat and reached his hand out to me. "I don't think we can."

Slowly, I shut the laptop, then took his hand so he could help me stand, and he led me back to his bunk. This was the moment that I had to decide if I was going to go with whatever he wanted us to do or turn back.

I was going with it.

He helped me into his bunk then climbed in behind me and shut the curtain. It was dark with only the glow of the dim light in the corner. All the bunks had them.

"You tell me to stop and I stop," he said. I nodded.

With London, I felt safe in knowing that he was all about my consent. He wouldn't do anything that I didn't want done.

When he kissed me, though, it became even clearer that there wasn't anything he could want to do that I didn't want.

We kissed and he lay me back. His hands wandered first to my breast on top of my shirt, then underneath. He squeezed and ran his thumb over my hard nipple then groaned. His mouth moved from mine to that thumb, where he sucked and ran his flat tongue over me.

It didn't take much to get me needy and urgent.

All of the sex I'd experienced before had been very polite and by the way he kept moving a little farther down my body, I knew I was about to experience something I hadn't before. No one had ever done this to me because again, it had all been very polite, missionary sex.

He slid my pajama bottoms down and ran his tongue over my clit, and I discovered that I'd been missing out. Or maybe it was just with him that I could ever feel this way because there was no doubt that London was quite skillful.

London massaged me with his tongue. He licked harder, then lighter without me saying a word. It was like he already knew exactly what I needed as he worked his magic. I tried not to look down at him. Tried so hard because if I did, it would be over. I wanted the release but didn't want him to stop.

Maybe it was that I'd been on the edge since he'd kissed me or maybe he was *that* good, but within what felt like minutes, I was coming with his mouth on my clit and two of his fingers inside me.

Slowly, he pulled out of me then was back beside me with his arm wrapped around my waist, kissing up my neck until he found my lips again. It took me who-knew-how-long to catch my breath, but when I did, I opened my eyes to find him looking down at me with softness in his eyes.

"That was—"

"I know." He ran a hand over my hair. "You're fucking beautiful when you cum, Charlotte."

The burning in my face was immediate. Given what he'd just been doing, this shouldn't have embarrassed me, yet it did. Then he fell back over onto his back and I got the impression that this was done.

"Wait," I said quietly. "I thought that was the beginning, not the end."

He rolled back over and stroked his thumb over my hot cheek. "That was for you since I got you all worked up earlier, but I'm not having sex with you on this bus. When I have sex with you, I don't want you to think you have to be quiet. I want you to be free to make all the sounds you need to without covering your mouth."

"I covered my mouth?" I asked. He nodded. "I didn't realize that."

He smiled. "I know."

"Wait. You said *when* you have sex with me."

He chuckled quietly. "It kind of feels inevitable, doesn't it?"

That, it did.

I lay there in just my tank top until his breathing evened out. Then I got dressed and slipped out of his bunk and back into mine.

The only problem was that because of London, I still couldn't fall asleep.

11

LONDON

I was fucked.

Now that I'd had a taste of Charlotte, I was starved for more. I could've fucked her last night. She'd been willing. So why in the holy hell had I said *no*?

Easy answer.

Because I wanted time to explore her body. To make her feel all the things that I could make her feel.

Because I knew that the moment I had her, I wouldn't want to let her go.

Like I said. I was fucked.

When I hopped out of my bunk, we were already in Chicago. It was a quick trip. We had two shows here and would get two nights in the hotel before a couple of days off then Detroit. That meant I had four days with Charlotte and even if she stayed in bed with me all of those days, it wouldn't be enough.

It'd never be enough. I hadn't felt like this since Holly and because of that, I needed to stay away from Charlotte before I was in too deep to get myself out.

Yet I couldn't go the entire rest of my life without knowing what it was like to have sex with her.

Nobody had ever said my brain wasn't a fucked-up place to be.

"Where is everybody?" I asked Lilah because she was the only one out in the main area when I got out there.

"I think Jamison and Thatcher are still asleep. Grayson, Lennox, Kenzie, and Becca went to get coffee and I think Charlotte is also still asleep. I haven't seen her."

The urge to immediately turn around and crawl into that bunk with Charlotte was almost over-whelming.

There was something wrong with me.

"Oh, Sean stopped by before they left and said he'd be back with the keys to our rooms at the hotel. He's getting us checked in and all that. Should be anytime now, so you'll be able to get to your room soon."

Most of the time when we were staying in hotels, Sean got our keys, then we just headed there when we wanted to. It was always a really early check-in and we didn't give a shit about any extra cost. It was worth it to shower in a real shower that I didn't have to share with four other guys.

"The girls are going to stay in Becca's room," she told me, and I hadn't thought about the fact that we had extra passengers but not extra rooms. "It seemed easiest since I'll be staying in Grayson's."

Jealousy tore through me. Not that I cared much where she was staying, but the fact that Grayson got to have her with him and Charlotte would be in a room with her friends and not me.

This was so fucked up. Technically, I barely knew Charlotte, and yet in a matter of days, I already didn't want her to leave. It didn't make sense.

"You know we all see it, right?" Lilah's words surprised the hell out of me, though I tried not to show it.

"See what? What do you think you see?"

Her face was soft and I hated that. It was the face kind of caring face that I used to get. "That you're falling for Charlotte."

"The fuck I am."

She sighed. "Listen, I don't know why you are the way you are. I've only known you a little while and my boyfriend won't say shit about anything. He just says you don't have girlfriends."

The muscles that had tightened as soon as she said she didn't know why I was the way I was relaxed at knowing that Grayson didn't tell her all of my business. "Good. At least he can keep his mouth shut."

"And I get the whole 'rock star thing' or whatever. But you like her. Clearly, she likes you. Why not grab what you want in front of you?"

"Because there's nothing more than surface-deep I want in front of me." I took a step closer. "Maybe I'll see if she wants to fuck in a van behind the venue then never see her again. That worked for you, right?" That was such an asshole thing to say to her. Lilah and Grayson had hooked up one night after a show when we were still playing bars.

I never judged women who filled their needs with one-night stands or anything else. Hell, without women willing to have one-nighters, I'd never have sex. I just didn't want her in my business.

The door to the bus opened and Grayson

climbed on but stopped when he saw Lilah's face. It was hard with hurt painted all over it.

"Why does my girlfriend look like that?" he asked, holding back the anger I could see wanted out.

"Don't worry about it," she said, but she kept her eyes on me. "London's just upset."

Fuck right I was. "She looks like that because I reminded her that not everyone wants a relationship. For some of us, fucking in a van is good enough."

"Are you fucking kidding me?" he raged.

"Sorry, brother. But she needs to keep her nose in her own business instead of trying to marry me off to some woman whom I don't give two shits about."

"London," Lilah whispered, then she nodded her head to something behind me.

Some*one*. Charlotte was standing there with big, round eyes of surprise. She had that just-woke-up disheveled hair, partly from what I'd done to her last night, and not a grain of makeup on. I would say this was the most beautiful I'd ever seen her.

"I'm going to get dressed," she said quietly, then she turned and climbed back into her bunk.

I closed my eyes and mouthed the word "fuck."

But I wouldn't let Lilah or Grayson know that I was upset with myself. They didn't need that boost to their egos.

"Anything else you need from me?" I snapped at Lilah.

"You're an asshole, London," she finally said, then she turned toward the door.

"You're just figuring that out?" I called after her.

Grayson hadn't moved, his muscles tense. "What's wrong with you?"

"You know what's wrong with me."

"Yeah. I do. And it's time you got over it. Through it. Whatever. You closed yourself off a long time ago. I get it. We all do shit to protect ourselves, but you were just downright mean not only to my woman, but to yours."

"She's not my woman." But fuck did I want her to be even if I wouldn't fully admit it to myself. The idea of Charlotte being mine made my chest swell but the thought of what could happen if I let myself care for her was stronger than anything else.

"Well, she won't be now. You can keep telling yourself that you don't feel anything, that you don't want anything from her. That's fine. You can even miss the chance to be happy, but you don't have to be a fucking asshole about something that's entirely your choice."

Before I could reply, Charlotte's curtain slid open and there was movement behind me. It took everything in me not turn and look at her. Then she slipped by and headed out the door. Grayson waited until she was out before he shook his head.

"You're an idiot."

"Are you just figuring that out now?"

"No. I'm just learning the extent. Apologize to Lilah."

Then he was gone too.

The worst part of all of this was that Grayson was right. I fucking hated it when he was right. Lilah didn't deserve the way I'd talked to her and until I found her to apologize, Grayson was going to pissed at me too.

As much as I wanted to be the asshole I knew I needed to be, in this case, it wasn't the best idea.

Finding Lilah was my first priority, even though everything in me said to go to Charlotte first. But I'd likely ruined any chance I had with her—and maybe that wasn't a bad thing. I'd already gone too far with her.

It didn't take long to track Lilah down. She was in the dressing room making sure our outfits for tonight weren't wrinkled and laughing with Becca as if nothing else had just happened.

"Hey," I said as I came to a stop near them. They'd ignored me coming into the room, which meant that Lilah had told Becca that I'd been an asshole. But had she told her the details?

"Is there something we can help you with?" Becca asked when Lilah didn't turn around.

Yup. She knew about my behavior.

"I'd like to talk to Lilah."

"Then talk. She's right there." Becca pointed at her best friend and I knew I wasn't going to do this without one pint-sized audience member hanging on to every word.

"What did you tell her?" I asked Lilah.

"She told me you are being an asshole, though try as I might, I couldn't get out of her why," said Becca.

Well, at least there was that.

"Lilah," I said more gently, which made her face me finally. "I'm sorry for the way I acted on the bus."

"Are you apologizing because you're really sorry or because Grayson told you to?" Lilah asked with her arms crossed under her breasts.

"Both?" It came out sounding like a question,

which made the corners of Lilah's mouth twitch. "I'm sorry. Some things are a sore subject with me."

"Obviously." She contemplated me for a minute then gave a single nod. "Apology accepted. Thank you."

My job here was done, but Becca couldn't let it go.

"That's it. He apologizes and he's forgiven, but you won't even tell me what this is about?" She sounded like a pouting kid more than anything.

"That's how it works," Lilah told her then turned to me again. "I have a question, though. You don't have to answer it."

I'd known this was coming. "Go ahead."

"Why are you so sensitive about anyone suggesting you might want a relationship?"

"Because I don't want one. Anything else?"

Lilah rolled her eyes at me then shook her head.

If I wasn't going to tell Charlotte why I didn't do relationships, I sure as hell wasn't going to tell Lilah or Becca. Though it was good to see that Grayson hadn't told her. He'd witnessed the aftermath of Holly and promised to keep my confidence.

Good to see that he was.

Right before our soundcheck, Sean asked us all to follow him into the closest room. It had long tables and lots of chairs. I assumed this was where catering came in and people ate. Right now, it was empty.

"What's up?" I asked once we were all in there. Jamison sat in the nearest chair while Grayson and I leaned back against a table, my hand gripping the edge. Lennox and Thatcher stood closest to the door and Sean was in the middle of us all.

"I received an interesting call this morning," he said. Well, that could go either way. "From the Governor of Michigan."

"What?" all of us said at the same time. That wasn't what any one of us had expected him to say.

"Why would the Governor of Michigan call you?" I asked, already knowing that I wasn't going to like the answer.

"Well, apparently, he's looking for his daughter."

"What's that got to do with us?" Jamison tipped back in his chair as he stretched.

"It seems like she's on tour with us."

"Say that again?" Grayson glanced at me because it was obvious who he was talking about. We all lived in Michigan and knew our governor's last name but didn't assume that Charlotte's last name being Andersen meant she had to be the governor's daughter. Now we knew.

"I guess she left school a few days ago and hasn't been back to her apartment. Her friend's car was towed from the side of a highway. I guess he tracked it down to the garage it was taken to. But somehow, they were able to track her to our shows and he wanted to know if we'd seen her. And since he knows she's been to multiple shows, he wanted to know if we have any information about her following the tour."

I closed my eyes and kept the slew of swear words at bay, though they wanted to rip through the air like a knife.

"How did they find out about her being here?" I asked.

Sean shrugged. "Don't know. The guy did say something about some emails that make them think she and her friend would be here though."

"Charlotte?" Grayson asked for confirmation, though both of us knew he didn't need it.

"Yup. I told him I'd look into it and call back," Sean explained. "But let's be clear here. He already knows the answer. He wouldn't have reached out if he didn't."

"What's Charlotte's last name?" Lennox asked.

"Andersen," I told him, though I shouldn't have.

"Damn."

"Anyway, he wants to send some people to get her and bring her home." His eyes locked with mine. "If I have any information."

"You don't." The words flew out of my mouth before I could stop them. I didn't want her to leave at all, but certainly not that way. She'd said they'd find the car. I just hadn't asked questions after that. I looked at Grayson. "I've never seen her use her phone. Have you?" I asked. He shook his head. "Seems to me she doesn't want him to contact her, then."

"I think you're right," Sean agreed. "How do you want to handle this?"

Everyone could probably assume why he was asking me that question and at this point, I didn't care. "I don't." He furrowed his brows. "I don't think any of us should let her know we know who she is." Then I turned to Sean since he was the one who would have to deal with the governor. "I also don't think we should have any information to give him."

"Got it. I'll tell him I couldn't find anything."

The rest of them headed to soundcheck and it took me maybe half a minute to follow. Charlotte being the governor's daughter didn't throw me. He always came off as a huge asshole in his press conferences that I'd seen, but I didn't give a shit about that. But there were ideas floating around in my head as to why she'd leave her family without telling them where she was. Like she was running and that didn't sit well in my stomach.

Now I had two reasons I needed to talk to her.

After soundcheck, I wanted to be alone but go get something to eat. There was a lot of together time on the road and normally, it didn't bother me. It was like a group of brothers with the band, but right now, I wanted to be an only child.

There were usually places to eat within walking distances from the venue and in Chicago, I could count on it. This was a great place for walking. I let Sean know that I was leaving so they didn't worry when they couldn't find me—like I said, a family. Then I headed out.

I was about a block away when I noticed Charlotte walking by herself, an act that didn't sit right with me. Keeping my distance, I watched her, lost in thought, as she strolled along in her far-too-sexy sundress. It was short, showing off those smooth legs. The memory of those legs against my cheeks when I'd gone down on her made my dick harden. I was walking on the streets of Chicago with half a woody.

Damn my body and its reaction to this woman.

But when she almost stepped off the curb when the light told her to stop, I couldn't just follow her anymore. I reached out and grabbed her arm to pull her back.

Surprised blue eyes looked up at me.

"What're you doing?" I asked more harshly than necessary.

She blinked three times before answering. "I was lost in thought. Thanks." We stood too close together for too long. "What are you doing out here? Were you following me?"

I shook my head. "I was headed to get something to eat and happened to see you. Want to join me?"

"Do *you* want me to join you?"

Everyone around us began moving, indicating that the light had changed. Still, I stood there with Charlotte.

"Yes."

She bit down on her bottom lip as she thought about her answer. Charlotte had every right to reject me right now given that this whole thing hadn't gone totally smoothly. "OK, then. Let's find somewhere to eat."

We went into the first place we came to and found a seat by the door. It was a cozy little restaurant with a menu that ensured us we were going to have the best sandwiches in the world.

Once we'd ordered, we sat in mostly awkward silence. I needed to start this conversation but didn't know how. Turned out, I didn't need to. I opened my mouth to speak when Charlotte beat me to it.

"Do I really mean nothing to you?"

12

CHARLOTTE

I couldn't believe the words had come out of my mouth the way they had. Talk about diving into the deep end.

"Sorry," I said right after, though I wasn't. "Wait. No, I'm not." I adjusted in my seat while London tried to form some words.

"Listen," I started. "We haven't known each other very long, so it's not like I thought I'd mean the world to you, but I thought we were friends. Or becoming friends and after..." My cheeks heated at the thought of mentioning what he'd done. "Last night, I thought... I guess I don't know what I thought, but I really didn't expect to hear you say that I don't mean shit to you. Was I wrong about all this?"

"No," he finally said. "You weren't wrong." He took a drink of his coffee before continuing, as if that was the liquid courage he'd needed, though there was no alcohol in it. "I'm sorry, Charlotte. I never should've said that. I'll explain, but know that I'm not trying to make excuses."

I nodded so he'd know that I heard him, but this was the first time I'd seen London look uncomfortable. Admittedly, I hadn't known him long, but he dripped with confidence in everything I'd seen him do.

"Lilah insinuated that I have feelings for you and should act on them." His brown eyes glanced to my lips then back. "But I don't do feelings. I fuck. There's no easy way to say that."

"I'm not that delicate, London."

"OK. It's just sometimes women—never mind. Anyway, I don't do feelings and I don't do relationships, as I told you."

"Yes. You were very honest about that."

"Well, when Lilah said it, the asshole in me kicked in and I was saying all of that to her. It wasn't really about you."

"But it *was* about me. That much was clear." Much clearer than his explanation.

"Yeah." He ran a hand through his hair and

paused for the waitress to set our order on the table. Though my stomach hated the idea of eating, it would give me something to do. "I'm sorry about that."

"You've already said that."

"I know." He took a big bite of his sandwich, so I picked my ham and cheese up to take one too. A smaller one. "Anyway, I was trying to make sure she'd never say it again because..."

"Because?" I raised an eyebrow.

"Because I don't do relationships and don't want anyone thinking otherwise. People get hurt that way."

It was clear to me that he wasn't going to tell me why he was the way he was and it wouldn't be right for me to pry. Clearly, something or someone had hurt him in the past. In a way that was going to take him time to heal from, if he ever did. It wasn't my place to try to push him or change him. That had never been my intention.

My intention had been to have some fun. Do something for me. Not live the life my parents had planned for me.

"Well, there's good news, London. I wasn't trying to be your girlfriend. Or trick you into a relationship."

"I know you weren't. This wasn't about you at all."

"Then let's forget about it, but try not to refer to me and 'shit' in the same conversation again." I shrugged. "It hurt my feelings."

"I'm sorry."

I rolled my eyes. "Stop apologizing. I already accepted your apology."

We each took another bite. Suddenly, I was hungrier than I had been.

"Fine. I will," he agreed. "I think I was a bit more on edge after last night."

My chest and cheeks flared with heat that I knew he would see. This shouldn't have embarrassed me and it wasn't exactly.

"I guess we just shouldn't do that again." Saying those words caused me pain.

Last night had been a new experience for me and maybe somewhere deep down, I'd hoped to experience it again. If that wasn't in the cards, it wasn't in the cards.

"That would be a fucking shame." The intensity in his eyes warmed me in a completely different way.

But London was so confusing. He didn't want me, or at least a relationship with me, but he seemed to want my body.

I thought that was an arrangement I could live with.

When I went back home to my real life, the one that included polite sexual partners who didn't do what he'd done last night, I'd be able to look back on this week fondly. It could be that thing I'd done once. I'd had a moment with rock star. Not every woman could say that.

I just wondered if—*when* I went back to that life, if it would be with a broken heart. Especially considering I might see him again if he kept his promise of donating to the shelter that I was now determined to open. I mean, even my father should've been agreeable to it, given that it was still helping and the argument could be made would look very good if I ever ran for office. Which I wouldn't. I would still be doing something that would make him look good, even if that wasn't the reason I was doing it.

"I just meant—"

He cut me off. "I know what you meant. I also meant that it'd be a fucking shame. You're beautiful when you cum and I'd like to see that again."

My eyes widened like tea saucers as I leaned across the table and put my hand over his mouth. "Are you insane? People can hear you."

"I don't care," he said from behind my hand.

"I do." Or at least I cared if someone happened to record it and it got out.

Ugh. I was growing really tired of worrying about what might become public for the sake of my parents.

I just wanted to live my life.

"Sorry." He chuckled, which meant he wasn't sorry at all.

"Not forgiven on that one."

That only made him laugh louder. It was an infectious laugh that I had to fight not to join in.

He shrugged. "You seemed to enjoy it."

Biting the inside of my cheek was the only thing keeping a big, stupid grin from forming. "Hard not to when someone does something new to me and does it so well." No idea where that had come from. Usually, I wasn't so forthcoming. Usually, I didn't have anything to be so forthcoming *about*.

His brows slammed down in confusion. "Something new?"

Well, I'd backed myself into that corner. "Nothing."

He leaned in closer and dropped his voice. "Are you telling me no one's ever gone down on you before?"

Now the real embarrassment kicked in. "We don't need to talk about this."

"I think we do because if you're a virgin, you should've told me."

"I'm not a virgin!" My voice traveled a bit further than I'd intended, making the man at the closest table raise his eyebrows as he looked at me. I closed my eyes and hoped the rest of the restaurant would disappear before I opened them. Unfortunately, they didn't. "I'm not a virgin," I said more quietly. "It's just that all of my experiences have been very polite."

"*Polite?*" He spat the word as if it were poison.

"Polite," I repeated. "Polite enough that it didn't include... that. OK?"

He stammered as he tried to form a sentence. I guessed I could render London Kerr speechless. "I guess I'm glad that I'm *impolite.*"

I brought my knuckles to my mouth to hide my smile. "I guess I am too," I finally said.

He reached out and covered my hand that was on top of the table with his and ran his thumb over my skin. It was a nice gesture. An intimate one, which only confused me more.

"Can you do me a favor?" he asked. I nodded. "Can you not talk about you with anyone else again? I've got a jealous streak."

My stomach tightened. "Good thing I'm not your girlfriend, then. You don't get to have a jealous streak."

"I still get to have it," he countered. "Which is bad enough. I don't get to act on it, which is worse."

London Kerr was going to drive me crazy. In good ways and some not-so-good ones.

We left the restaurant soon after to make the walk back to the venue. London wrapped his arm around my shoulders and I told myself it was a friendly thing to do, but Kenzie had never done that to me, so how friendly could it have been? I wouldn't ask, though. No way. That would spook him or at least it could and that was the last thing I wanted. Instead, I was going to enjoy the sensation.

With the venue up ahead, I thought we'd go directly there, but London turned us into the parking lot to a secluded corner that was blocked in by buses. It was as private as possible. Probably more private than inside the actual bus.

He didn't say anything before wrapping his arm around my waist to pull me into him. His other hand pushed into my hair before his lips claimed mine.

Kissing London was like no other kissing I'd ever experienced. Not surprising. Polite sex comes with polite kisses. The biggest difference was that London wasn't worried about how my father would react if he caught us or if he'd done something wrong.

That was the worst part of my family's criminal history. Their money had been made in shady ways that came with a body count. That was my father's grandpa and his dad for a while. Though his dad had worked hard to change that image and so had my father. The knowledge still lingered, though.

I braced my hands against his chest and melted into him. His tongue ran across my lips, asking for permission that I readily gave. He tilted my head back to deepen the kiss that I felt to my toes. If he would've wanted to have sex right there, I can't say that I would've said *no*. And when he brought the kiss to an end, I was left breathless and aching. Again.

Something that didn't go unnoticed by him.

"I fucking love that a kiss makes you so needy." His lips brushed against mine.

It was true, even if it was embarrassing. "Polite sex, remember?"

He growled at the mention of my past. "I bet you're so fucking wet."

"I bet you're right." Where this person, this version of me, had come from, I had no idea. There was no way I could match London's dirty talk, so I wasn't trying. But somewhere along the way, I decided that with him, I wouldn't be reserved. After all, there were only four more days until Kenzie and I went back home and I faced the music.

"You're fucking killing me." His hand slid up the outside of my thigh, under my dress, until his reached my panties.

Then his fingers gently walked up and slid inside. My breath caught in my chest when he ran a fingertip over my clit and my legs spread slightly on their own. I sure hadn't told them to do that. London walked me back until I was against the side of a bus. My eyes were closed as he worked his magic, but I could feel him watching me.

He'd said I was beautiful when I had an orgasm, so I had to assume that was what he was watching for. When his wet mouth hit my neck, my eyelids popped open and both of my hands slid into his hair. His breath quickened as if he were getting as much out of this as I was, but there was no way he could've been.

Two fingers pushed into me as his thumb worked my clit. "I was right." The words came out like a groan, but I knew what he was talking about. Once again, it should've embarrassed me yet didn't.

Right now there was only one thing I cared about, and that thing hit me like a freight train.

Before I could cover my mouth so no one would hear me, London kissed me again, swallowing all of my moans as he kept pushing me over that edge.

Once I fell off and landed, he kissed down my neck and slowly pulled his fingers from my pussy, righted my panties, and let my skirt fall back into place. Then he rested his forehead against my shoulder as I gently ran my fingers through his hair.

We were like that for who-knew-how-long before he finally stood back up.

London's hair was disheveled thanks to my fingers and I could feel the heat on my skin. I was hotter than I should've been, even in this warm temperature.

"Fuck," he whispered, which filled me emotion.

The fact that I seemed to affect him the way he did me was unexpected and powerful. We might've only had a few days left, but there was no way we weren't going to have sex before then.

"I have to go," he said, but the fire was still in his eyes.

"I know."

"Come on." He waved his fingers at me and the sudden embarrassment of the fact that those fingers had just been inside me hit. "Don't worry about it," he said, as if he knew what I was feeling. "Let's go so I can get ready for the show."

"Go ahead. I can come in after you."

"Fuck that. I'm not leaving you our here alone. Come on."

I nodded and hurried over to him, though this time, he didn't put his arm around me, which I missed, or take my hand.

"I can't believe I just let you do that somewhere anyone could've seen us," I whispered. We were walking quicker than I would've liked because that meant we'd be around the others sooner.

London stopped before the door. "I wouldn't let anyone see you." When I tried to protest, he spoke first. "If anyone would've seen anything, they would've seen me." He stepped closer. "I wouldn't put you in that position, Charlotte." He glanced at my lips and then back. "I won't let anyone near you who you don't want to be near you."

That was a weird promise to make, considering at the moment, there was only one person I was kind of hiding from and he had no idea about that.

"Now let's go get ready for the show."

London opened the door to the venue and held it for me to pass through. Now was the time to act normal again. As if nothing had passed between the two of us.

I hadn't even told Kenzie about last night and wasn't sure that I would. If I was going to do...well, whatever I was doing with London, I thought I'd keep it just for me.

She knew we'd kissed and that was enough.

I couldn't believe we were going to pull this off. Though I hated the fact that I only had a limited time with them. Four more days. Tonight and tomorrow's show in Chicago, two days off, then we were back to Detroit, where we'd go our separate ways.

I was beginning to hate the idea of Detroit.

13

LONDON

Walking into the area after making Charlotte come and have to have to act like nothing happened fucking killed me.

I wanted to take her back to the bus and fuck her all night. Or the hotel since we were staying in one tonight. *Fuck.* I'd forgotten to take my stuff to the hotel. Whatever. I'd do that after the show. After all, the hotel was basically next door. It'd be a quick walk.

Charlotte was right in front of me when she stopped short, almost causing me to slam into her back. It wasn't her fault. Sean had quickly stepped out from one of the rooms so suddenly, it was that or plow into him.

"Oh, good. You're both here. Everyone's waiting in the dressing room."

Charlotte glanced back at me. "Waiting for what?" I asked.

"The two of you to get here. I got some news."

I raised an eyebrow. "If it's about what you found out earlier—"

"It's not." He cut me off and gave me a nod of understanding that meant he wasn't going to say anything about that. "Come on."

Charlotte shrugged then followed Sean into the room with me on her trail. He wasn't kidding when he'd said everyone was waiting inside. The guys were scattered around the room, all in different stages of getting ready. Lilah and Becca were leaning against the wall on the other side with Kenzie not far from them. Charlotte made a beeline over to her friend, which left me by the door.

"What's up?" I asked, hoping that my earlier assumption wasn't wrong. That he wasn't about to tell everyone what we'd learned about Charlotte earlier. Though why would he? We all already knew.

"I got a call from the venue in Detroit. They had a big storm roll through last night that caused significant damage."

"That sucks," Jamison said. "What's that got to do with us?"

Sean turned toward him. "We can't play there in four days. It's going to take about week to get the place back up to snuff."

"So we cancel?" Lennox asked.

"We cancel," Sean agreed. "Usually, we'd reschedule it for later in the tour, but you have a couple of days off next week and we're still in this general area. It'd be tight, but I think it would be better to get it done ASAP. So we could reschedule Saturday and Sunday's Detroit shows to Friday and Saturday of next week. What do you guys think?"

The general murmuring through the room seemed to be in agreement, so I told him, "We all agree with that."

"It'd mean you wouldn't really have any days off next week."

I shrugged. "After the two this week, they were a luxury anyway."

He nodded. "Good. I'll set that up. I already asked and the venue doesn't have anything scheduled those days."

"Why did they need to be here?" Jamison pointed at Charlotte and Kenzie, making Sean look back to me though he was talking to Jamison.

"I wanted them to know about it because they're supposed to be with us until Detroit. This makes Detroit a week later, so if they want to make arrangements to go home after the shows in Chicago, I can help them out with that."

Unconsciously, I looked at Charlotte. Probably a mistake, to be honest, but I had to see what she was thinking. The last thing I wanted was for her to leave and if I had any say in it, she'd stay until Detroit like she'd planned. They had tickets for Detroit. To me, it just made sense.

"Uh..." Charlotte glanced at her friend.

"I want to stay until Detroit," Kenzie said without discussing it with Charlotte. "But I also don't want us to be a pain in your ass or have you let us keep tagging along when you don't want us to."

"You're not a pain in *my* ass," Jamison said. "It already feels like you're part of the tour, so I have no problem with it."

"We want you to stay." Lilah piped up. "Becca and I like having other girls here with us. Plus, we've already become friends."

My chest was tight as Charlotte worked her bottom lip trying to decide whether she should stay or go home. When she finally looked at me, I mouthed *stay* because she and I weren't done yet.

She tucked a piece of hair behind her ear and nodded. "If it's no trouble..."

"It's not," Sean told her, which I was thankful for. I'd been about to say the same thing and really shouldn't have. "You can just stay in with Becca if that's OK with her."

"Fine by me," Becca agreed. "We should have a slumber party tonight."

Lilah smiled in excitement. "Yes!"

"No." Grayson's voice came out louder than anyone else's.

"Why not?"

Hi adorably grumpy face was all scrunched up. "I don't get you in an actual bed very often, that's why."

He was right. He didn't and truth be told, I wanted Charlotte in mine tonight.

"Well, you all can fight over that." Sean headed for the door. "But remember after tomorrow, you're as free as birds for four days." Then he left.

"You know what we should do?" Lilah said once he was gone. "We should rent a beach house."

"Yes!" Becca agreed. "Maybe on Lake Michigan. Somewhere we can all just relax. It'd be fun."

And that's how it was decided that we were going to rent a beach house for four days. It sounded good to me. Touring could be stressful, so we had to take every chance we got to unwind. Sure, most people might think that since we're together all the time that maybe we'd all want to go our separate ways and we did. Sometimes. But again, like family, if the house was big enough, we might not even see each other.

The ladies were heading out of the room, so we could get ready and do our preshow shit. As she passed me, I couldn't miss the opportunity to brush my hand over Charlotte's. She shivered but kept walking.

The show went off without a hitch. Because we had another show here tomorrow night, we were done early and I headed to the hotel. I'd seen Charlotte in the audience, but not since. After a quick stop at the bus to grab some clothes, I walked over to the hotel with Jamison and Lennox. Those two were planning on going out. I wasn't. Mostly because I knew they were going to be hooking up tonight, which was great for them, but I wanted no part of it.

Our rooms were all pretty close to each other's, taking up the far end of the hallway. Though I didn't know where everyone's was, I could hear the giggles coming from the ladies' room. It would've been Becca and Lilah's, but Charlotte and Kenzie were in there too.

It wasn't too late, but I figured I'd watch some TV until I fell asleep. Except someone knocked on my door as I was stepping out of the shower. If that was Jamison...

I yanked the door open. Definitely not Jamison.

Charlotte stood in front of me in her regular pajamas. Shorts and a tank top, which would've been perfectly acceptable to be in out in the hallway in if she'd have put on a fucking bra.

She startled and stepped back. I had been a little aggressive in opening that door. As her gaze slid down my bare chest to where the towel was snug around my waist, I was reminded that I'd just gotten out of the shower and was mostly naked.

"Hey," I said with a little confusion. "Sorry. I wasn't expecting you to be on the other side of this door."

Her deep-blue eyes found mine. "Were you expecting someone else?"

"No," I said quickly. "I wasn't expecting anyone, but when you knocked, I thought you'd be Jamison trying to get me to go out tonight."

"You didn't want to go out."

"No." I shook my head then stepped aside. "Come in."

She slid past me and the smell of cherries came

with her. Her blonde hair was down but not done. As in there was no product, which meant that after the show, she must've left right away to come here to shower.

"You can have a seat if you want. I'll get dressed. I'll only be a minute."

Charlotte turned to me. "Do you not want to have sex with me?"

Did I just hear what I thought I heard? That couldn't have been a serious question. "What?"

Her fingers twisted back and forth around each other and her bare feet rubbed against one another. This woman was a conundrum. Shy sometimes. Bold others. Unable to spit out dirty words one minute. The other asking me if I wanted to have sex with her.

"Do you not want to have sex with me?" She spoke slower, as if I hadn't understood the first time.

"I think you know that I do. Why are you asking me that?"

"Because you haven't."

"We've been on the bus in those fucking small bunks."

"But today—"

"I'm not going to fuck outside against a bus."

"Are you saying you've never done that before?" The bolder she became, the less she fidgeted.

"I'm not saying that." Because I'd be lying. "I'm saying I'm not fucking *you* against a bus where anyone could see us." I moved over to her close enough that she had to look slightly up and I had to look down. "I think you know how hard you make me. I think you've felt it."

"But—"

"No *but*s," I said, cutting in. "I'm half fucking hard right now, Charlotte, just being near you."

"You are not." Clearly, she didn't believe me, so with one small movement, I dropped my towel.

"OK. Maybe three-quarters."

Those big, blue eyes widened and her skin pinked up as her fingers covered her mouth.

"I... You..." She stammered and I tried not to laugh.

She definitely hadn't been expecting that.

"What's the next move?" I asked her because this whole thing was up to her. She knew where my boundaries lay. I wouldn't cross those, but if she was up to fucking without strings, I'd take her up on it. She'd go into it knowing it wasn't going to lead anywhere. "If it were up to me, you'd already be on that bed and I'd already be inside you. But this isn't up to me, Charlotte."

"What if I'm not good at it?" she asked with hesitation. "Polite sex, remember?"

I groaned. Despite having asked her not to bring up her being with someone else, I couldn't fault her. She was worried she wouldn't be good enough for me. That was funny, given that all I needed was for her to be there and it'd be perfect.

"I'm not worried," I told her quietly. Besides, anything she wanted to learn that wasn't so polite, I'd teach her if she wanted me to.

"I am."

"Don't be." I took another step closer. If I got any closer, my dick would bump into her stomach. "But if you're uncomfortable, Charlotte, just say so. We don't have to do this."

"I want to." That was the most certain of anything I'd ever heard her be.

"Do you want 'polite'?"

Her teeth sunk into her bottom lip as she looked up at me, then she slowly shook her head *no*.

Fuck. I was in trouble.

I wrapped my hand around the back of her neck and pulled her close to me so that I could give her a kiss she wouldn't forget.

Since I was already naked, I needed to her that way, too.

As our tongues battled for the dominance that I was so easily winning, I only broke the connection long enough to lift her shirt over her head. Her bare tits pressed against my bare stomach as I pushed her shorts and panties to the floor. Then I moved us over to the bed.

I would've love nothing more than to push my cock into her hot mouth, but she was already feeling insecure about her abilities, so I wasn't going to do it. We could work on that next time.

Instead, I moved her to the middle of the bed and settled between her legs. The warmth from her pussy made me shiver, but I cautioned myself not to move too quickly.

Kissing down her neck to between her breasts, I left a wet trail, marking all the places that I'd already been. Her nails scraped against my skin when I stuck my tongue out and licked her nipple. My girl was responsive. Maybe because she didn't really know what it was like to be fucked.

She would when I was done.

I squeezed her tits as I made my way down to the promise land. Charlotte didn't hesitate opening her legs for me. I had to fight a grin. I'd done this to her last night and clearly, she was wanting more.

I'd give it to her.

As I licked her from back to front, the muscles in her legs tightened against my head. Exactly the response that I'd wanted. Fuck going slow. I dove in, tasting her and savoring before zoning in on her clit. This time, when she tried to cover her mouth, I pulled her arm down to the bed.

"Keep it there," I said, then I licked her again. She'd have to do it herself because my hands were busy. One cupped a breast and squeezed while I pushed one finger from the other hand into her. I could stay down here all day, but alas, there was a higher purpose to this. I licked and sucked, moaning because I didn't care if she knew how much I enjoyed this. Actually, I *wanted* her to know.

I also wasn't quiet about it. She didn't want polite, so I wasn't going to worry about it.

The room was filled with the sounds of my work and her pleasure, which built into the orgasm that hit quickly. It could've been that she just came easily, but I was taking all that fucking credit.

While she was still distracted, I grabbed a condom from my bag—never leave home without them—and rolled it on. Back between her legs, I didn't waste a second. This was what I'd been fucking yearning for.

As I kissed her, I pushed inside of her and took the surprise that escaped her mouth as mine. Finally, her head fell back as I found my rhythm. Her legs tightened and her nails dug into my back. If I was lucky, she'd leave a mark.

Just when I thought she was going to cum again, I pulled out, which got me a pout.

"Turn over," I told her.

Her eyes widened, but she did it. I positioned her up on her hands and knees then slowly slid into her from behind.

"Fuck," I muttered. She was so fucking tight from this angle, I didn't think I'd be able to hold on. She'd been tight the other way, but this was next level.

Charlotte moaned then dropped her forehead to the bed, her arms shaking as she tried to stay up on them. She was going to be sore in the morning.

This time, when I pulled out, she whimpered. "On your back."

She collapsed onto the mattress, where I could climb back over her.

This time, I moved a little more slowly. The end was coming and I didn't want to. I mean, I did want it to because it felt fucking fantastic. But I didn't want to because being inside her felt fucking fantastic.

Finally, I couldn't hold out any longer and I spilled into the condom.

Both of our breathing was erratic, with short gasps for air. When I felt like I could, I slowly pulled out of her, careful to hold on to the condom. After kissing her again, I hurried to the bathroom to take care of it then was back beside her, under the covers with her Jell-O-like limbs curled up next to me. I pulled her into me and wrapped an arm around her.

"That definitely wasn't polite," she said quietly.

"You didn't want it to be, remember?" I said. She nodded. "You're all right, right?" Again, she nodded.

"I literally had no idea it could be that way."

"Yeah, baby, it can be." As I held her close, I asked, "Did you really think that I didn't want you?"

Her shoulders lifted then dropped. "It seemed like you didn't."

"I always want you, Charlotte. I want all of you." In a whisper, I added, "That's the fucking problem."

14

CHARLOTTE

I snuck out of London's room not long after he fell asleep, regardless of how much I wanted to stay with him all night. It wasn't a good idea. Girlfriends spent the night. I wasn't that to him and wouldn't pretend otherwise.

But every sexual contact I had with London was better than the last and it was going to be sad when it ended.

Becca and Kenzie were both asleep when I tiptoed in. Thankfully. The last thing I wanted to do was have a thousand questions pelted at me the second I'd stepped through the door. Especially when I didn't think London wanted anyone to know about us. This way, I got to carefully get into bed with Kenzie and replay every moment over and over until I finally fell asleep.

The movement in the room woke me long before I was ready to get up. As I opened my weary eyes, I found Kenzie and Becca both packing up their things.

"Why are you two happy so early?" I asked, my voice sounding like gravel in a blender.

"It's not that early." Kenzie threw a pillow at me. "We have to get moving for checkout."

I shot up quickly. "Do I have time for a shower?"

"If you hurry and don't worry about drying your hair."

I flung the blanket off me. "I'll put it in a bun."

"What's that?" She pointed at me, but I had no idea what she was talking about.

"What?"

"Where did you sneak off to last night?" she asked instead of answering me.

"Nowhere. I just went for a walk." The lie slid out of my mouth so easily that I almost choked on it. I really had to ask London if he minded me telling Kenzie. I didn't like lying to her and she wouldn't tell anyone. At first, I'd thought I wouldn't tell anyone anything but now that this had happened, I really wanted to talk to my best friend about it.

"On your collarbone." She squinted from where she was at the end of the bed. "It's like a red blotch."

"Oh." My fingers went to my collarbone, though I had no idea where the offending mark was. "I must've slept on my hand or something."

"Uh-huh." She didn't believe me, but I didn't have time to convince her. After being with London last night, I really needed a shower.

Fifteen minutes later, I was dressed in shorts and a tank top with my hair in a bun and Converses on my feet, ready to go to the venue. The girls had waited for me, so the three of us headed out together. Though we ran into Grayson and Lilah in the hallway to make it five.

I couldn't help glancing back at London's door before stepping on the elevator, wondering if he was still asleep or what he was doing. As the door closed, a hand shot out, forcing it to open back up.

London stepped in, causing me to move to the side to allow room. He and his bag brushed past me then slid behind. My spine straightened knowing he was there. His bag tapped my leg, so I knew he was close, then his knuckles dragged down my arm, which was on the other side of everyone else. Little things that no one would've seen. Simple touches that had me on heightened alert. Again.

He'd said a general *good morning* to all of us when he stepped on, but we were all quiet on the ride to the lobby. Once we were outside, that changed.

"I found us a great rental on Lake Michigan," Lilah told us. "It's going to be four relaxing, glorious days."

"And it's huge," Grayson added. "We figured everyone would want some room after being cramped on the bus."

Lilah groaned. "It is huge and beautiful, but it's expensive. He insisted."

Grayson chuckled. "I told you not to worry about it."

She shrugged. "It's your credit card."

When we got to the bus, everyone dropped off their stuff and shuffled off. I went to follow the girls, but London motioned for me to hang back until they were gone and we were alone on the bus. I was by the hallway and him by the door when they'd emptied out.

"Good morning," he said with more meaning than he had in the elevator.

"Morning." I tried to sound cheerful and friendly, which was what I thought he'd want.

"Where were you this morning?"

I furrowed my brows. "Sleeping."

"You weren't in my room when I woke up."

Oh. It was surprising that he cared. "I didn't think you'd want me to be." I quickly wet my bottom lip. "Girlfriends spend the night, London. Hookups leave when the hookup is done. Or that's what Kenzie told me during her hookups." That reminded me. "Oh, and what are your feelings on me telling Kenzie where I was last night? I lied this morning and don't feel good about it. She's my best friend and won't tell anyone."

With every word I spoke, London got closer until he was right in front of me and I stopped talking.

"I don't care what you tell your friend. I never asked you to lie."

"I know, but—"

"I'm not hiding you, Charlotte." He ran his hands down my arms. "Do I want the entire band to know? No. I don't. But that's not because of you, that's because of them. We'd never hear the end of it because—"

"They'd think I was your girlfriend and you don't do girlfriends. You don't want to have to say something like you did to Lilah."

He nodded. "Something like that."

"OK. Got it."

He hooked my chin between his thumb and finger, pinching just hard enough to pull it forward to kiss me. This wasn't like last night's kiss, though I still felt it everywhere. London had the uncanny ability to make the rest of the world disappear with the slightest touch.

When he pulled back, he ran his thumb over the red spot—the mark he'd left there—which was a lot lighter than it had been this morning and said, "Good Morning." Again. I liked this one better.

"Good morning."

"Now I have some band things I have to go do."

"I understand."

One more quick kiss and he left.

With everyone busy, Kenzie and I thought it a good time to do a little exploring. We'd both been to Chicago before and loved it, so we hopped a ride share and headed to Millennium Park. It was a great place to walk around and there was still so much to see.

And a lot of time to talk.

"I lied about where I was last night," I told her.

She turned to me with wide eyes. "What? You lied? Are you serious?" She was totally deadpanning all of that.

"Knock it off." I nudged her with my shoulder. "I

wasn't sure I should tell you. I didn't know if he wanted anyone to know."

"By 'he,' I assume you mean London."

"Yes."

"Was he good?" she asked. "I feel like he'd be good."

"Wouldn't they all be? I mean, they've probably had the practice."

"True." She took a drink from the water she was carrying. "It'd be kind of sad if they were bad after all this time, right?"

Our fit of giggles had people looking at us.

"But, yes. He was good. Impolite."

"Impolite?" she repeated. She'd know exactly what I was saying. "Big day for you."

"I know." Luckily, we could laugh through this and she wasn't mad that I'd lied earlier.

"Does this mean the two of you are together? I really wouldn't mind my best friend being a rock star's girlfriend."

"No." I sighed, trying to hide any disappointment that I felt. "He doesn't do relationships and that's fine. We're here for about a week more, assuming my father doesn't catch up to us, and then this will just be an amazing memory. Though I'm probably ruined for whatever son of a friend my parents have ordained that I marry."

Kenzie stopped, grabbed my arm so I would, too, and turned me. "You are *not* marrying some 'polite' bastard who doesn't know how to give you an orgasm. I'll kidnap you first."

I shook my head, knowing that she'd do it, too. "No. I'm not. Once I graduate, they're not going to determine my path." I started walking again. "Oh, I told London about wanting to open an animal shelter and he wants to help. Says the band is always looking for a cause. If that ends up happening, I might not have to limit it to dogs and cats. Eventually, I could get more land and take horses." I toss my hands in the air. "Anything is possible."

"I love this for you, Charlotte, and I'm going to be there with you helping any way that I can."

I knew she would be. She was my best friend.

Kenzie and I wasted our day in the best ways possible. We were gone almost all the way until showtime, which meant we didn't see the band or Lilah and Becca beforehand. It wasn't until we were all on the bus that we were together again.

Some of the guys were at the table. Lennox was in the single chair playing the PlayStation. London was on one end of the couch, me in the middle, and

Becca next to me. Poor Lilah was squeezed in between Grayson and Jamison at the table. The table could've fit more people, but the guys took up a lot of space. There were legs everywhere.

Kenzie came out after putting her pajamas on to find that there wasn't really anywhere available. Except the floor.

"You can have my spot," London said as he pushed to his feet. When he moved, though, I slid over so she could have my spot because he was dropping to the floor with his back against Jamison's chair and his legs stretched out in front of him.

"Thanks," Kenzie said to him. Then she got a little devilish grin. "Wouldn't want you to be *impolite*."

I bit my lips together and felt the blood rush to my head. It didn't seem to bother London. He just smiled and said, "Actually, I enjoy being incredibly impolite."

"I've heard that about you."

He chuckled as I tried to melt back into my seat.

Well, now he knew I'd told her.

The bus was taking us to the house Lilah had rented that was near Grand Haven, Michigan on the shores of Lake Michigan. She promised it'd be beautiful and once we stocked the fridge, it would be amazing.

No one seemed tired and there were so many conversations happening at once. Kenzie and I were telling Becca about school, though I was careful to leave out any of the stories that included my "babysitter," Donovan. Kenzie talked a lot about the parties we'd go to, though I'd still always had a shadow. She told Becca about the time she'd had to hobble back to the apartment drunk and had gone into the apartment below us to see the couple who lived there in a very compromising position that had included three other people.

I'd told her she'd imagined it, but she swore it was true.

"Real barnyard stuff," Kenzie said to Becca.

I scrunched up my nose. "Barnyard stuff? I don't want to hear the details."

The bus roared with laughter.

The topics changed, the conversations moved. I sat back, feeling a little sleepy, to listen to them all. I was leaning my back against the arm and the next thing I knew, I was awoken by a bump in the road.

The main area was void of anyone else and dark. Apparently, everyone had gone to sleep and left me out there. Though I did have a blanket tucked around me. Even with as comfortable as I was, I decided I should go to bed. After tossing the blanket off me with the intention of heading to my bunk, the bus hit another big bump as I stood up, sending me to the ground.

No. It wasn't the ground. It was hard muscle. I'd fallen off the couch onto one of the guys.

How embarrassing. He had his head to the side, so I couldn't tell who it was, so as gently as possible, I placed my hands on the floor on either side of him and started pushing up. Big hands wrapped around my arms and pulled me back to him.

"Where are you going?" London's tired voice asked.

"I... The bus hit a bump and I fell."

"I didn't ask why you're on top of me. You can be here any time you want. I asked where you were going."

That was right. He had. "Bed. I must've fallen asleep on the couch."

"You did." He reached out to pull his blanket back then draped it over me. The heat from his body was a welcome change to the cool air. The bus was rather chilly at night, on purpose, to make it more comfortable to sleep. My bare legs slid against his.

His chest was also bare, so he must've been in boxers.

After he wrapped his arms around me, I asked, "What are you doing out here?"

"Didn't want to leave you out here alone."

I bit the corner of my mouth to keep from commenting. He might not have thought about how damn sweet that was or what everyone else might have thought if they saw us.

"What?" he asked. I shook my head. "You look like you have something to say. Say it."

I took a deep breath. "That's sweet of you to stay out here with me." I swallowed hard. "That's a boyfriend move. For someone who doesn't want to be a boyfriend, you're pretty good at it."

He shook his head. "It's not that I don't want to be your boyfriend. It's that I *can't* be."

"I wasn't pushing. You wanted to know what I was thinking," I said. We both grew quiet before I asked, "Do you think you might tell me why? It won't change anything. I promise. I won't suddenly decide that I can fix you or anything. I'm curious, though."

"Yeah. I'm guessing I probably will tell you because when you leave the tour in Detroit, I suspect it's going to be harder for me than I think."

15

LONDON

I lay with Charlotte as long as I dared. Just her on top me as I ran my hand over her hair.

This was bad. Real bad. I was getting too fucking attached and I knew it yet couldn't stop myself. Whenever she was near me, I wanted to touch her. I didn't, but I wanted to.

When the bus slowed like our driver had gotten off the highway, I planned to nudge Charlotte, but she pushed herself off me before I had the chance. Like she knew it was time to go to her bunk because the others might come out here.

It wouldn't have been a big deal if someone saw us, but I'd never hear the end of it.

"Time to go to bed," she said without prompting,

but as soon as her body weight was gone, I missed it. I could've slept like that.

"I suppose so."

After getting up off the floor, I tossed the blanket I'd been using onto the couch with hers then followed her to the bunks. I gave her a quick kiss goodnight, though I wanted it to be more, and waited for her to get into her bunk before climbing into mine.

It was hard to get back to sleep, but eventually, sleep won out.

I woke the next morning to silence. As in, it didn't sound like there was another person on the bus and once I dropped out of my bunk, I realized there wasn't. We were parked in front of this huge house, so everyone was probably in there. After getting dressed and brushing my teeth, I packed up everything I'd need for four days.

Out in the main area, the divider was pulled back where our driver, Kelly, sat flipping through a magazine.

"Got everything you need?" he asked.

"Yeah, I think so."

"I was just waiting for you. If you have everything, I can head home for a few days."

"You should've woken me up."

He scowled at me, though that was mostly his permanent facial expression. Still, he was a nice enough guy. "I can wait."

"I'm good. You're sure everyone else has what they need?"

"That's what they said."

I gave him a little nod of acknowledgement. "Have a good break."

He snorted, but as soon as I shut the door behind me, he drove away.

The house was white and looked like it belonged somewhere else. Large entryway that led me to the kitchen, where Grayson, Kenzie, Becca, and Lilah were laughing about something someone had just said. I hadn't caught it.

"Look who decided to wake up," Lilah said when she saw me.

Trying not to be obvious, I glanced around looking for Charlotte, but she wasn't here with them. "Someone could've woken me up."

"Nah," Grayson countered. "You needed your beauty sleep."

"The fuck I do. I'm naturally beautiful," I said. Lilah was scribbling on a piece of paper. "What're you doing?"

"Making a list. There's nothing to eat here, so we're going to the grocery store."

"I need some things. I'll go with you." I pulled my phone out to check the time. "Where do I put my shit?"

Lilah squinted like she was trying to see something that wasn't there. "Fourth door on the right. Up the stairs. You were last off the bus, so you get the room that was left."

"I don't care where I sleep."

"I've heard that about you," Becca quipped, which got her a firm middle finger in the air.

"I'll be right down, then we can go Uber?"

"Nah," Grayson told me. "Lilah had a rental delivered for all of us to share. Thought it'd be easier."

It would be.

As I headed out of the kitchen, I thought my room might not be so easy to find. Right then, I couldn't find the fucking stairs.

"They're over here," Grayson said, suddenly behind me.

Looking to the right, I saw where he meant and went that way.

Up the stairs, he pointed to my room. "I can count," I told him.

"I wasn't sure and didn't want you to get lost."

"Fuck off."

We both chuckled.

The bedroom was large, like the house, everything white and wood, and it looked brand new. That bed could've slept five people minimum, but I was going to enjoy having it to myself. Or scratch that. Sharing it with Charlotte if she'd stay with me.

"What's going on with you and Charlotte?" Grayson asked and since we were the only two in the room, he didn't try to whisper.

"Nothing. Why?"

"I saw you sleeping on the floor of the bus next to her."

"She was on the couch."

"You know what I mean."

"Nothing. I mean, I like her. She's a decent person. But she's leaving in a week and you know I don't do relationships, so nothing's going on with us."

"Fine. Fine." He sighed. Grayson had been trying to get me over my issues for years. What he didn't understand was that I wasn't willing to open myself up to that kind of heartbreak again. "We'll leave as soon as you come down."

Unpacking wasn't a priority, but seeing Charlotte

was. Realizing how much I wanted to see her when it'd only been a few hours made me that much more relieved that she was leaving next week. Though I was beginning to think that wouldn't be soon enough if I hoped to come out of this unscathed.

It was hard when I got back downstairs to see Charlotte and now feel like I could make contact. I had in the elevator yesterday, but no one could see that. Or I didn't think they could.

Realistically, no one would've cared if I was with Charlotte. The guys didn't give a shit whom we all fucked. Sisters were out and that was the extent of it. The problem was me and I knew it. I'd shut off that part of me a long time ago because losing someone you love was hard and I wouldn't do that shit again.

"Ready?" Grayson asked. I nodded.

He had the key, so he slid in behind the wheel with Lilah in the passenger side. Which left Charlotte and me in the backseat. Fine by me. I wasn't afraid to be around her. I could be normal.

The car Lilah had rented was large enough to accommodate eight people by my estimate, but it was unlikely that we'd all be going anywhere together. Still, it was nice to have the leg room.

Grayson followed the GPS to the nearest store, which was one of those supercenters, and Lilah grabbed a cart while pulling out her list. No idea what was on it.

"We have to eat for four days," Lilah began, taking control of the situation. "And Jamison wants to grill every night. So we need that stuff and then regular staples. Snacks. Drinks."

Charlotte pulled out a second cart. "Why don't I take half the list and you take the other? It'll get done faster."

"Good idea." Lilah tore the paper in half. "And get anything you and Kenzie might want. Any snack that might sound good. These guys can eat a lot."

Charlotte snickered, glanced and me quickly, and then headed in the other direction, leaving me with Grayson and Lilah. Grayson raised an eyebrow, which made me shake my head then follow after Charlotte.

"You're in a hurry," I told her when I caught up. The grocery store was empty enough that none of us had gotten stopped yet. It usually happened and there was no guarantee it wouldn't today but so far, it hadn't.

"No, I'm not." She glanced up at me as she put bread in the cart. "I mean, I don't intend to grocery shop all day because it's not fun shopping, but I wasn't in a hurry."

"You walked away without me."

"I didn't know you were coming with me."

That earned her a scowl. "Yes, you did."

She stopped and turned to me. "OK. Maybe I did. But it's confusing to me. Do you want people to know that we're... whatever we're doing? Or not? I thought I was being normal. Friendly."

"You were." I just didn't like it. "Listen." I put my hand on the cart to stop it. "I don't care what people know. The guys have seen me with women before," I said. Her jaw clenched, reminding me that I might not catch feelings, but Charlotte could. Even if she was willing to walk away from them when we got to Detroit. "That's not what I meant." I sighed. "I meant, that just because they see me with you doesn't mean they'll think we're together. They know that's not going to happen."

Charlotte swallowed hard then pushed the cart away from me. "OK."

The kicker was, there was no tone. Nothing in her voice that said she was upset. Just another thing to love about that woman. I'd told her my boundaries and she was working within them. There'd been no trying to convince me or trying to change me.

She was happy to be take what I could give.

"So what do you like to eat?" she asked when we were near the snack aisle.

"You."

Her steps stopped and she turned to me. "I can't believe you said that near the Little Debbies."

"Nothing Debbie hasn't heard before."

Charlotte cocked her head to the side. "I'm sorry. You're mistaken. Little Debbie is an innocent. She doesn't need to hear your dirty mouth."

I stepped into Charlotte's space, close enough that our bodies were almost touching. "It wasn't for her. It was for you and I suspect you like my dirty mouth."

"Of course I do," she said quietly. "I'm just thinking of Little Debbie."

A loud laugh bubbled up from my chest, which caused her to break as well.

One thing I could count on Charlotte for was that we'd be fine.

In the past, when a woman had wanted attachment and I'd told her *no*, she'd do everything in her power to change my mind. She'd think if she gave me the best blowjob of my life that I'd completely turned around. It never worked, but I appreciated the effort.

With her, I almost wanted her to change me and

she wasn't even trying to. Therefore, she was giving me exactly what I wanted.

So why did I feel disappointed?

We finished up the list and added a shit ton of other things. Things I knew the guys would like, things she knew that Kenzie would want. Then we headed to the checkout, where Lilah and Grayson were in front of us.

"Jamison wants to do steak tonight," Grayson told me.

"Works for me."

"Can he cook?" Charlotte asked. "I'm not the best cook, so I won't be much help."

"He can cook," I told her. "He might be a lot of things, but the man knows how to grill. Grayson and I can cook too, so we'll be the backup."

Her eyebrows furrowed. "You two cook?"

"I didn't say that. We don't cook often because where the fuck would we do that?" Being on the road meant there was nowhere and we were so busy when we were home too. Cooking was a luxury that we didn't get to do often.

"But we can." Grayson finished my thought for me. "Our mothers made sure that we would be able to cook for our women one day." He raised his voice to mimic my mother. "'I'm not sending you boys out into the world for some poor woman to have to take care of.'"

Chuckling, I explained. "That was supposed to be my mom. Grayson was at my house a lot, so she treated him like her own. And it was her life's mission to make sure we wouldn't be a burden to anyone else."

"She succeeded and my mom was the same way."

Nodding, I looked back at Charlotte.

"Your mothers are very smart," she told us.

"They are," Lilah agreed.

Once we paid for everything and packed it into the SUV, Grayson followed the GPS back to the beach house.

This place was amazing and it had me thinking that I wanted some place like this. It didn't have to be as big or as flashy, but someplace out of the way near a beach sounded perfect.

Unpacking was my least favorite thing to do, but with the four of us, Kenzie, and Becca, it went quickly.

"I'm going into the water," Kenzie announced. "I don't have a swimsuit, but I don't care. Who's with me?"

"Are you going in naked?" Charlotte asked and I

couldn't guess if she was going to be down for nudity herself or not. My guess was not, but she'd been getting bold, so I wasn't sure.

"I have an extra suit you can borrow, Kenzie," Becca offered. "We're basically the same size. I'm sure it will fit."

"If you don't mind," Kenzie said.

"I have one you could use, Charlotte," Lilah added. "If you want to go in."

"I do," Charlotte replied.

With the women out of the room and only Grayson and me left, he asked, "You going to be able to control your sword with her in a bikini?"

"Bikini?"

He shrugged. "Lilah only wears bikinis that I know of."

Fuck my life. But not really. I'd seen what was under the bikini, so seeing her in one shouldn't have been a big deal.

Except I knew that he had a point. I'd have to figure out a way to keep from being obvious how fucking much I wanted that woman.

16

CHARLOTTE

"You need a bikini that color," Kenzie called from the bathroom attached to our room.

I'd already showered the lake off and was dressing for tonight. Jamison had started the grill already and the sun was making its decent into the horizon. It wasn't late yet, though, so there was plenty of light left for dinner. Probably a few hours' worth.

"I might have one. I just never wear them. We never go swimming."

"I'm just saying, red is your color."

Kenzie stepped out of the bathroom, a billow of steam following her out. I'd already finished putting on this cute sundress that I loved. It was pink and hugged my body while at the same time being flowy. I hadn't gotten my hair wet in the lake, so I didn't need to wash it, but the bun I'd been wearing gave me these great waves that I loved.

I felt very much like I was at the beach.

When we joined everyone else out on the deck, dinner was already done. There was a big, oval table that would accommodate all of us and still have room for the food. Lilah and Becca had insisted that they had the sides handled, as if we were their guests who shouldn't help out.

I sure didn't feel like a guest at this point. I felt like I'd known these people all my life.

There was a spread of summer salads and fresh veggies to go with the steaks Jamison was pulling off the grill. He dropped one on my plate that could feed several people at once.

"That's too big," I told him.

"That's what she said," Lennox added, making me shake my head at him like a kindergarten teacher chastising her student.

"*Mazel*," Jamison said, patting London's shoulder as he passed him.

"The fuck that's supposed to mean?" I didn't think London was asking about what Jamison said.

"You two are fucking, aren't you?" Thatcher asked, causing my skin to heat.

"Don't talk about her like that," London countered.

"See?" Lennox pointed out. "None of us care. She's here for a week, now two, so it was probably going to happen."

"What was going to happen?" I asked.

"Listen." Jamison dropped into his seat. "You're beautiful women. We're guys. It was kind of inevitable."

"Why?" Kenzie countered. "No one's fucking me."

"Or me," Becca agreed. "And that's not an offer or a request."

"Same." Kenzie pointed at Becca in agreement.

I couldn't believe what was happening right now. They were talking about sex like it was an everyday, normal topic of discussion. This was so weird to me and thank the universe for Lilah.

"Anyway..." she said, clearing her throat. "Have you two ever been to this part of the state?"

"No," Kenzie said right away. "But Charlotte has, I'm sure. She's been everywhere."

"Not for fun," I reminded her.

"True. But you've still been everywhere."

"Your family travels a lot?" Lilah asked.

"You could say that. It's mostly for my dad's job." I took a deep breath then looked around. "The food looks delicious."

Once the subject changed, I could enjoy the dinner they'd made. Though the steak really was too big.

Kenzie and I wouldn't let them shoo us away from cleaning up. We wanted to help in some way. We got the dishwasher loaded then everyone filed back out to the deck. But the night was too beautiful for me to just sit there.

"I'm going for a walk down the beach," I told them as I stood.

"You shouldn't go alone." Kenzie got up from her seat.

"I'm a big girl."

"I'm well aware. But it's night time. What if the Loch Ness Monster comes out of the water and takes you away?"

I cracked a smile. "There are so many things wrong with what you just said, but how would you being with me help in that situation? If a monster came out of the lake to snatch me, what would you do?"

"Record the event for prosperity."

The two of us began laughing, but I knew she was tired. She'd said so earlier. "Just stay here and relax. I'm fine."

"I'll go with her." London was already on his feet and his offer had Kenzie falling back into her chair.

"Good," said Kenzie, fanning herself, "because I don't think I could walk ten feet. I'm about to have a food baby."

Every single one of us laughed probably because we were all feeling the exact same way.

We were surrounded by sand, so I didn't go in for shoes. Barefoot was just fine for me.

London was wearing khaki shorts and a black T-shirt. He kicked his shoes off on the deck before stepping out into the sand. We walked close to each other without touching until we were away from the house a little. Then he took his hand in mine.

It was the first time he'd held my hand and I had the immediate thought that I never wanted to let go.

Maybe this whole thing was stupid. And maybe I'd break my own heart when it was time to leave, but I wouldn't regret my time with London no matter what else happened.

This was the first time I felt like my own person and knew that there was more out there. And he was responsible for that.

"It's such a beautiful night," I said quietly as we walked in the wet sand near the water.

"It is." He stopped, so I did too, then he turned to face me.

London cupped my cheeks then leaned down, our lips brushing lightly before he fully kissed me. It was slow and gentle. Not like some of our others. His tongue worked its magic with long, languid strokes.

Damn him for having this effect on me. One kiss and I'd gladly get naked in the sand.

I couldn't even imagine that. One picture by a random stranger and my world would crash all around me.

I brought the kiss to an end and blurted out, "I have to tell you something."

He was still holding my face with his head tilted to the side. The end of that kiss had been a surprise to him.

"OK." He stood up straight, trailing his hands down my arms until he could hold mine. "You can tell me anything."

I swallowed hard. This wasn't some deep, dark secret I was about to confess to. Nothing like that at all. Yet for some reason, admitting that I'd avoided telling anyone why I couldn't let my family find me felt pretty much like that.

"To be clear, Kenzie and I weren't running away from anything."

"I didn't think you were." His brows were pinched in slightly like he was really worried about what I was going to tell him.

"My parents are fairly controlling and sneaking away from school was the only way we could have this week. We needed this. *I* needed it. The Forever 18 shows were just an excuse."

A smile played on his lips. "Are you saying you don't like us?"

"No," I said too loudly. "We love you." *Damn it.* "I mean the band. We love the band. Kenzie had tickets for Detroit and we wanted to do something unexpected, so she suggested we go to all of your shows this week. Then her car broke down and you know the rest."

I took a moment for air.

"I don't know if you'll remember this or not, but when you guys picked us up, I said that they'd find her car once we had it towed. 'They' are my parents. Or my father specifically." Another deep breath. "He's the Governor of Michigan. I have a babysitter named Donovan who follows me every freaking where. To make sure I'm safe, according to my dad, but it's really to make sure I don't do anything to embarrass the family. They're very big on appearances."

His eyes squinted. "Didn't I hear something during the election about a colored past or something?"

"Yes." I sighed. "That's why he's obsessed with appearances. His grandfather was basically a mobster. Something about the unions and I don't even know all of it because I don't want to. See, my grandfather decided he wanted to clean up the family image and groomed my dad for politics. He's going to run for president."

"Seriously?"

I nodded. "I hope he doesn't win, to be honest, but now my dad is grooming me for politics and I don't want that."

"You're opening your animal shelter."

"Exactly, but I have to play the game until I graduate because he pays my tuition. Once I'm done, I get my trust fund from my grandfather and can tell my father and his plan to go to hell. I mean, I technically have access to it now but everything goes through him. Once I graduate that won't be the case."

"Wait. Is that the grandfather you were in the accident with?" he asked.

I shook my head. "My mother's father and I were in the accident and the trust fund comes from him, actually. Unfortunately, he put my mother in charge of it, and she put my dad in charge of it."

"Was his grandfather's name Bugsy?" he asked, trying to keep a straight face.

I snorted. "No. It's not funny, London." Though it kind of was. "It's just a lot of pressure and a lot of not being free."

"I'm sorry." He wrapped his arms around my shoulders and pulled me to him. I folded mine around his back and buried my face in his chest. Taking a deep breath, I promised myself to remember what he smelled like. Laundry soap from his clothes and fresh, clean soap. There was something else I couldn't put my finger on but assumed that was him.

Pulling back, I told him, "I just wanted you to know. No surprises."

His body stiffened and he stepped away from me before running his fingers through his hair. Then he nodded for me to follow. "I feel like this will be easier if I'm moving."

"OK." But there was so much confusion in me that I didn't know where to start.

"I told you I don't do relationships."

"I remember."

"And I told you I'd probably tell you why eventually."

"You did."

He took a deep breath then blew it out quickly. "I had a girlfriend in high school. We were together, like, three years. Planning on staying together after. She was it for me."

My stomach tightened both because clearly, this story didn't have a happy ending, but also out of jealousy. Jealous that this unknown woman had a part of him that I never would.

"I know people say shit about high school love being transient and all that, but it was real and no one could ever convince me it wasn't."

"Of course not," I told him. "Your feelings are real no matter how old you are when you feel them."

As if I hadn't spoken, he continued, though he looked out at the water as he did and not at me. "Her name was Holly. We went to our senior prom then an afterparty. She was such a good girl. Didn't ever step out of line. She also had epilepsy but hadn't had a seizure in years. I mean *years*."

The urge to reach out to London as he bared his greatest heartbreak was almost overwhelming. I couldn't, though. Or rather, I shouldn't. I didn't think he'd like that.

"We went to this afterparty and she wanted to be a regular teenager for a change, so she had a few drinks. I didn't because someone needed to get her home safe and I wouldn't put her at risk like that. So she had a few drinks. Didn't even go overboard, then I took her home. At some point during the night, she had a massive seizure. Fell. Hit her head. She died alone on her bedroom floor."

My breath caught in my chest. "That's terrible," I told him quietly. "I'm so sorry."

"Yeah. Turns out alcohol mixed with her meds was a bad idea. I didn't know. I don't know if she did." He swallowed hard. I only noticed because I was watching him so closely. "Her mom said that alcohol lessens the med in her system or something, which gave her the seizure. No one knows why she was up. If she hadn't been, she might still be alive. Or maybe not. Seizures can be deadly on their own. Who knows?"

The silence between us hung there and I didn't like it.

"I'm sorry, London. I don't know what else to say to make it better."

"There is nothing anyone can say." He stopped,

only now there was a strong set to his chin. "It was years ago. I'm over it."

I tilted my head to the side. Was he? "How can you be? It sounds like if that hadn't happened, you'd be living a life with her. Probably married."

"Maybe. No one knows what would've happened after high school. Charlotte." He leaned down so that we were more at eye level. "I'm not pining for my dead girlfriend. I'm not. I don't want you to think that. It took a long time, but I'm past that now. It was seven years ago. Of course a small part of me will always love her, but that's not what this is about."

"Then what's it about?"

"This is why I can't be with you. Not in any real way. That fucking sucked and I won't ever go through that kind of pain again. I can't."

That did explain things a little more clearly. "I understand, London. I'm not asking you to. I've never asked you to. I've just been enjoying what we're doing."

"I know!" he yelled, but it wasn't directed at me. He was yelling at the universe. "I know you're not." His voice got a lot quieter. "I know you're not asking for anything, Charlotte, but you're the first woman I've met since then who's made me even consider it and that scares the shit out of me."

"We can stop having sex," I said quietly. I didn't want that, but I didn't want to see him like this. In pain.

"I sure as fuck don't want that, either."

At this point, I didn't think he knew what he wanted. I could only go on what *I* wanted. Or what I was feeling.

And all I was feeling was him.

17

LONDON

Telling Charlotte about Holly made me feel both better and worse.

She tried not to show it, but her eyes gave her away. It had made her sad and I suspected it was because of what had happened, yes, but also because she knew that I was serious about not ever having someone I loved like that again.

It didn't make sense to other people, but I didn't need it to. This was what I had to do to protect myself.

But I was also serious about continuing to have sex with her if she was game for it. Being inside Charlotte was like being at peace.

No matter how "impolite" I might've been.

I'd never hear that word again without smiling.

We were gone long enough that the sun had fully set, and there was a fire up by the house—a small campfire that I assume Jamison or Lennox had started. We made our way back, coming close enough to see that Grayson and Lilah weren't out there any longer. Didn't need two guesses to figure out where they were.

They were in the same place that I wanted to be with Charlotte. A bed. Hey, our time was limited. I wanted to spend as much of it with her as I could.

We approached the deck, my arm around her shoulders, pulling her into me, yet not a single person was surprised.

"We started a fire," Jamison said, stating the obvious, though the slowness of his words told me he'd had a fair share of beer since I'd been gone.

"Are any of you sober?" I glanced around.

"I am," Becca and Kenzie answered at the same time, then they giggled.

Becca continued. "I thought it best for someone to be stone-cold sober if these fools were going to play with fire."

"Good thinking." That had been what I was worried about. That I wasn't going to be able to get Charlotte inside due to needing to take care of that fire. I leaned down to whisper in Charlotte's ear. "What do you want to do? Stay out here or—"

"Go inside." She cut me off, bringing a smile to my face.

"We're going inside," I told the group as I let my arm fall off her shoulders so I could take her hand. It'd been a long-ass time since I'd held a woman's hand before Charlotte.

As I led her across the deck, we were almost to the sliding door when Kenzie called out, "Make sure you're *impolite*."

I snorted, but Charlotte groaned.

"Always am," I called back.

"Why would he impolite?" Jamison asked.

"Yeah," Lennox continued. "If he wants to fuck her, he can't be impolite." Their voices got farther away, but we could still hear them.

Lastly, Kenzie told the guys, "Just focus on your fire. You wouldn't understand."

Once we were in my room and the door was shut, I turned to Charlotte. "At least Kenzie's looking out for you."

She snorted. "Yes. She always wants what's best for me," she said. I pulled her over to the bed, took a seat, and rested my hands on her hips. "She was always encouraging me to find someone to... 'fuck the good girl out' of me. Direct quote."

I groaned. "And you never took her advice?"

She shook her head as her gaze met mine. "Not until recently."

Bam. I was as hard as a rock. Sure, I'd been halfway there already, but Charlotte standing over me with her long, blonde hair falling over her shoulders and those deep-blue eyes trying to see my soul as she told me that I was the only one who got to fuck the good girl out of her had me ready to Hulk out of my shorts.

I stood, forcing her back a step, reached down to grab her thighs, then lifted. She squealed and held on.

"I guess I'll have to see what I can do," I told her.

Walking us over to the bed, I dropped her gently on the mattress.

Fuck, I was going to miss this when she was gone. Pushing all those thoughts and anything that could resemble a feeling away, I did what I knew how to do.

I kissed Charlotte, long and firm, while quickly pushing her dress up and yanking her panties down. Trailing my fingers between her legs, I found her wet and ready, but this wasn't going to be like that. I wanted her naked in my bed. I wanted to take time with her because right now, we had nothing but time.

There was no rush. We had all night and could sleep all day if necessary.

Reaching back, I yanked my shirt over my head then leaned back over her to taste that soft skin on her chest. The swells of her breasts were falling out of her dress because she was lying down. Her fingers tightened in my hair.

After getting the dress up her body as far as I could while she was on her back, I scooped an arm around her back to lift her enough that I could get the rest of it off.

My girl was naked for me. I would've taken a picture if she'd let me, though I wouldn't ask. That wasn't Charlotte, so I'd have to make sure to commit every detail to memory. Especially since she wasn't "my girl." I'd slipped up thinking about her that way twice, I thought. I needed to be more careful.

I dropped to my knees, spreading her legs further and bringing her to the edge of the bed at the same time. She was so pretty and inviting that I couldn't help but lick her slowly. If this wasn't one of my favorite things to do already, it would've been with her.

Her back arched. Her fists clenched. She ran a hand down her stomach. All the while I couldn't keep my mouth off her, I also couldn't keep my eyes off her.

Charlotte was fucking beautiful. Everywhere.

She was coming on my mouth so quickly that I almost wished it'd taken longer. When I pulled back, I swiped a hand over my mouth then stood enough to kiss my way back up her. I scraped my teeth across her neck and she shivered.

I needed to get my pants off but hated to leave her.

When I pulled back to do that, she sat up. Her hair was already wild as she bit down on her lip.

"What?" My hands paused before pushing my pants down.

"What?" she asked back.

"You look... something. Like you're thinking. Do you want to stop?" I'd hate it, but I'd do it.

"No!" Her voice bounced around the room. My eager little minx wanted to make sure I knew she definitely didn't want to stop.

"Then what?"

Her cheeks pinked up, even though they were already flushed. I was going to like whatever she said. Anytime Charlotte blushed before saying something, I fucking loved what she said.

"Tell me," I murmured just loud enough for her to hear me.

"I told you about the polite sex."

"Yeah." Though I didn't love hearing about it when I was about to cum in my pants.

She tucked a piece of hair behind her ear and wouldn't meet my eye. "Well, because of that, there are definitely some things I haven't done that I've been curious about, but I've never been comfortable asking. Or telling." Her damn blue eyes met mine.

"Like what? Tell me. I promise you can't shock me."

"It's not about shocking you." The heat on her skin flared again. "It's embarrassing."

"You can't be embarrassed with me. I just had my tongue in your pussy. I think we're past that."

She slapped a hand over her face and groaned. "It still is." Instead of explaining, she pointed.

Right at my dick.

She could do anything with that she wanted.

I dropped my hands and motioned for her to go ahead.

With nervous hands, she reached out and finished what I'd started. My cock bounced out of my boxers and almost slapped her in the face. That hadn't been on purpose.

Her touch was tentative when she reached out and took my cock in her small hand. It wasn't even a firm grasp, but I had to stifle a groan. There were too many parts of this. She wanted to learn something with me, have me be the one to teach her, and she was fucking touching my dick.

This would become a problem quickly.

"I'm curious..." She didn't finish her sentence, probably because she wasn't used to asking for what she wanted.

I'd make that easy on her. "Do whatever you want. I'll let you know if it's uncomfortable."

She dropped her hand. "I don't know what I'm doing. I could hurt you."

"You couldn't. Trust me. I'm exerting all of my control to make sure I don't cum on your face and that was with you just touching me."

Her gaze hopped to mine and I swore her already-dark-blue eyes darkened.

That gave Charlotte a little confidence. She took me in her hand again, this time firmly. She stroked me up and down and I would've sworn I'd died and gone to heaven.

Or so I thought until her tongue pushed through her lips and she licked me from base to tip.

Yup. She was going to be the death of me.

She licked and kissed then took me in her mouth. It was slow and unsure, so I fisted my hand into her hair to help guide her.

Letting her do her thing was fucking hard and I waited as long as I could. But since I didn't want to cum in her mouth, I had to pull her back far too quickly.

We'd work on my stamina with that.

I had her back on the bed, a condom in place, pushing inside her so quickly, yet I thought I wasn't going to make it.

Being inside her calmed me. It still wasn't going to last long.

When I spilled inside her, she didn't seem to care about how long it had been.

We were both breathless and tired. After a quick trip to the bathroom for both of us, I pulled her into my chest.

"This time don't leave before morning," I told her tiredly.

"I won't." Charlotte rested her head on her hand, which was lying on my chest, watching me. "I have to tell you something."

"Have we told each other enough for today?"

She shook her head. "No."

"You can tell me anything, Charlotte."

She quickly wet her lips then swallowed hard. "You can stop yourself from loving me," she said quietly. "But you can't stop me from loving you."

"Charlotte—"

"I just want you to know that. Don't worry." Her voice was becoming stronger, more confident. "I'm not going to be swooning or constantly reminding you. I know what we're doing here. I just also know how I feel. It doesn't matter that it's ridiculous, given that we haven't known each other long at all. But I feel like I know you and I've felt the most at home ever here with you. Please don't ruin this moment for me."

My heart was in my stomach with her admission.

I'd fucking known spending time with her was a bad idea. I'd wanted her, but I hadn't wanted her to get hurt, which was why I'd been upfront about what I could be to her.

Still, I wouldn't ruin it for her, like she'd asked.

"I won't," I whispered. There was too much emotion in my voice for me to speak any louder.

She gave me a curt nod then snuggled back into my side before quickly falling asleep.

I couldn't fucking sleep. What she'd said haunted me.

Charlotte was right. I couldn't stop her from loving me. No matter how fucking much I wanted to be able to.

This was a recipe for a broken heart. For both of us.

Once I knew she was completely asleep, I slipped out of the bed, grabbed a pair of pajama pants that I almost never wore, slid them on, and headed down to the kitchen.

After grabbing a bottle of water from the fridge, I turned around to find Grayson sitting at the table. Hadn't noticed him when I'd come in.

"You're a fucking stalker," I told him.

He chuckled. "I was here the whole time."

"Turn a light on."

"The light above the sink is enough."

"What're you doing down here?" I twisted the cap then drained half the bottle.

"Couldn't get to sleep but didn't want to keep Lilah awake." He watched me with a knowing eye. "I think that's the same reason you're down here."

"Something like that."

"How's that all going?"

This was going to be hard to say, but I'd made my

rules a long time ago and wasn't going back now. "She's getting too attached."

"What?"

"Charlotte. She's getting too attached."

Grayson's jaw set, making that muscle there flex. I'd seen that with him before when he was getting angry.

"Are you fucking kidding me?" he asked, sounding like the exasperated dad they used to tell me I was. "You think *she's* getting too attached?"

"Yeah. Just some things she said tonight." That I certainly wasn't going to share.

"You're a fucking idiot."

I gave him a humorless laugh. "Tell me how you really feel."

Grayson took a deep breath then shook his head. "Not worth it." He stood from the table and walked away without another word.

My conversation with him made things clearer.

I needed to get some space between Charlotte and me before this got even more out of hand.

Before I opened myself up to be devastated again.

18

CHARLOTTE

When I woke the next morning, I was alone in London's bed.

At first, I thought he'd gotten up before me, but there was a feeling in the pit of my stomach and I just knew.

He hadn't slept in here at all.

Telling him that he couldn't stop me from loving him last night had obviously been the wrong choice. If only I could've kept my dumb mouth shut.

Well, I wasn't going to wallow. This was all temporary anyway, so if it ended before it was supposed to, I'd deal with it. I'd known what I'd been getting into with him. He'd been clear.

I hurriedly threw my dress on then grabbed anything else of mine in his room then scurried to my room. Kenzie wasn't there. She must've already been downstairs. Since I had no idea how late I'd slept, I wasn't surprised.

After a quick shower, I wasn't going to take the time to blow-dry my hair, instead going for a messy bun. That was the signature look of women my age, after all. And all that mess was out of my face.

Then I took a deep breath and headed down. I was going to see him eventually anyway.

The entire group was in the kitchen. It was loud enough that no one seemed to notice me at first.

Grayson, Lennox, Thatcher, and Jamison were laughing and talking almost all at the same time as they sat at the table. London was with them, but he wasn't talking or laughing. Just following along with the conversation.

Kenzie and Becca were sitting on stools at the breakfast nook giggling at something Lilah was showing them on her phone. I stood in the entryway until Kenzie noticed me and waved me over.

"Lilah's showing us some adorable pictures of her nephew. You'd just want to eat him up." Kenzie pulled me into her.

She and I had the kind of relationship that didn't need a lot of explanation. Something she saw on my face or in my eyes told her that I needed comfort.

"I told you I gave up cannibalism," I said dryly. "Too many calories."

The three of them laughed at that.

While I tried not to pay attention to what the boys were doing, Jamison left the room to lord-knew-where then came back.

"Charlotte, there's a man at the door for you," he told me as he continued over to take his seat.

"What?" I asked. So did London.

So he *did* know that I was there.

"Who is it?" I asked.

"Didn't tell me."

After a quick, silent conversation with Kenzie, I headed to the front door. When she began to slide off her stool, I shook my head.

There was only one person who would knock on that door asking for me and if I was about to get a serious dressing down, I didn't need an audience. As I left the kitchen, one of the chairs scraped against the floor, but I didn't look back to see whose it was.

It didn't matter anyway.

I paused to shake out my nervous hands before turning the doorknob. When I finally did, I wasn't surprised as to who was on the other side.

"Good morning, Charlotte." Donovan stood tall and intimidating, taking up most of the door frame.

Intimidating to me, at least. He'd never intimidated Kenzie.

"What are you doing here?"

"I've come to take you home."

"I'd rather stay."

He gave me the smile he used when he wanted me to know that he found me adorable. Like a little kid telling a story. "You know I can't let you do that."

"How did you even find me? I haven't used my phone or anything."

"There are ways. The band's been very helpful."

I wanted to throw up. *The band's been helpful?* How exactly had they been helpful? I had some guesses and thought it was London. I'd scared him last night and this was the punishment. He wanted me off the tour so he didn't have to deal with a love-struck woman. Or something like that.

I didn't know him very well after all.

"I'll give you ten minutes to get your things, Charlotte. Then I'm instructed to remove you from the house any way necessary." His eyes darkened. "I'd rather not do that."

Donovan's family had worked for my grandfather way back. That was how my father had known that he could be trusted. His family history was darker than mine and to this day, it was like they'd been born without a conscience.

"I'll get my things. You stay outside."

"I wasn't planning on coming in unless you made me."

I shut the door quietly then rested my forehead against it.

That wasn't how I'd wanted this to end.

London was standing not far from me with his hands over his chest and his brows furrowed. "Are you leaving with him?"

I threw my hands into the air. "I don't have a choice, London. Isn't that what you wanted? Isn't that why you called him here?"

His face twisted in fake confusion. Or I thought it was fake anyway. "The fuck you talking about? *Called* him here?"

"He said 'the band's been helpful.'" I stomped away. "You could've just said we weren't going to do whatever the hell this is anymore." Tears burned my eyes. "You didn't have to send me home."

"I didn't," he said louder. "I don't know what you're talking about here, Charlotte, but I didn't do a fucking thing."

"So after what I told you last night, you didn't think I was getting too attached?" I spat. He swallowed hard. "I wasn't. I was being honest, but I knew what this was. You didn't come to bed last night, right? After asking *me* to stay?" His silence was his answer. "That's what I thought. I'm sorry that I care for you, London. Scratch that. I'm not. I'm not sorry for caring about you. I'm sorry you couldn't care just enough about me to not send me home with that man."

Then I stomped past him back to the kitchen. This new development affected more than just me.

"It was Donovan," I blurted out to Kenzie, no longer caring who heard me.

"What?" She dropped the fork she'd been using to eat her eggs. "Why the fuck is he here?"

"I have to go home. Apparently, *the band's been really helpful* to my father in finding me."

Her face hardened. "What?"

"Listen." I stepped closer. "You don't have to go. This is about me. You can stay on the tour until Detroit like you planned."

"I'm not doing that."

"Kenzie. I don't want to mess up this once-in-a-lifetime thing for you."

She hopped off the stool and took my hands into her. "I'm your ride or die. I'm going."

There wouldn't be any talking her out of it and I knew it. This was how she was.

My friend always.

The two of us hurried upstairs to pack our bags. We didn't think either of us had left anything on the bus since we hadn't brought much to begin with, but if we had, it was dead to us now. I sure as hell didn't want to ask how to get it back.

Both of us knew that when Donovan said ten minutes, he'd started a timer and would break through that door to get me when the timer expired. Then my father's money would get him out of trouble. It had happened once freshman year and after that humiliation, I'd promised both of us that it wouldn't happen again. It was how they'd gotten me to follow the rules this whole time. Me knowing he'd take extreme measures if my father told him to.

Kenzie and I were back down to the kitchen with only a couple of minutes to spare as far as my estimation went. We didn't have a lot of time.

"I can't believe you're leaving," Becca said as she hugged me. "You have my number, so don't be a stranger."

"You too."

Then I had basically the same conversation with

Lilah before it was interrupted by a knock on the front door. That was my warning.

"We have to go," I told her. Then I looked to the table. "Bye, guys. Thank you for letting us tag along."

There was a rumble of words that I couldn't understand since they'd all spoken at the same time.

Only London was still standing at the entryway to kitchen. He put his arm out to stop me.

"You don't have to go with him," he said quietly.

Meeting his eyes, I told him, "Yes, I do."

"I didn't do this, Charlotte."

"It honestly doesn't even matter anymore. I have to go before he comes in here."

London wet his lips. "See you in Detroit?"

I let out a humorless laugh. "You'll see Kenzie in Detroit. Pretty sure I'm about to become a prisoner for a while."

Then I walked away because there wasn't anything else to do.

Donovan was right outside the door when I opened it and without a word, the three of us headed to the car waiting in the driveway. A big, black SUV of course because someone liked to pretend his job was important.

He took our bags to the back as Kenzie and I climbed into the back seat.

"It's only about two hours to Lansing," he said from behind the wheel. "Sit back and relax."

"Um, we live in Ann Arbor," Kenzie told him back. She was never afraid of speaking up and I loved her for it.

"You will go on to Ann Arbor after Lansing. Charlotte will be staying in Lansing for a while."

When she looked at me, I shrugged. That wasn't a surprise.

As I'd told London, I was becoming a prisoner for a while.

One more year and I could put all of this behind me.

She and I didn't talk much on the ride to my parents' house. There wasn't much to say and there were ears listening that would report everything back to my parents. If I was lucky, my father would play the "I'm disappointed" card rather that the pissed-off, angry one. I could take his disappointment because his opinion didn't mean much to me.

On the hour and a half ride to Lansing, for the first time since I'd left my apartment to go to that first concert, I pulled my phone out of my bag and turned it on. There were messages and emails that I'd ignore, but I quickly sent one to AJ to let him know what was going on.

His immediate response was that he was on his way to Lansing. Though he'd never get there before us since he was in Chicago in med school, I'd be glad to have him there.

The governor's mansion was ten thousand square feet of mansion that was perfectly put together for stately occasions. When the gates shut behind after we made it up the driveway, it was like a commentary on my life right now. Shut in. Trapped under the guise of security.

"What do you think is going to happen?" Kenzie asked after Donovan got out of the car at my parents' house.

"It's not like he's going to yell. Dad almost never yells, but I'm sure I'll get a nice, long lecture about what a disappointment I am." There was no point in delaying the inevitable, so I yanked the door handle and left the car, ready to face whatever was going to be thrown at me. Or pretending to be ready.

"If *you're* a disappointment, I feel sorry for my parents," she said as we headed toward the front door.

This wasn't the house I'd grown up in. This was the governor's mansion where we'd moved when my father's money had gotten him elected. There was also a summer residence on Mackinaw Island that we'd never used once while I'd been at home. No idea what my parents did when I was away and I didn't want to.

"You shouldn't be," I told her as we went through the front door. "You're not a disappointment because your parents are normal."

She snorted quietly. "That's so hard to believe that even divorced, my parents are considered stable."

"Believe it."

Kenzie followed me through the house to my father's study. There was no doubt that was where they were waiting for me. After a quick pause and a deep breath, I opened the door without knocking.

"What were you thinking?" my father started without so much as a greeting. He sat at his big desk with my mother in the chair across from it while I stood before them with Kenzie at my back.

At least I had her. And AJ once he arrived.

I got my looks from my mother. I'd been told so many times that I looked like a younger version of her with the same blonde hair that she always had, though now she colored the gray away. Everything about my father was dark from his hair and eyes to his personality.

"That I wanted to have a little fun?" I posed my

answer as a question because I couldn't explain what I'd been thinking.

They weren't interested in hearing that the life they'd laid out for me was suffocating. That on the road with Forever 18, I'd finally felt free. Like myself. And I found someone whom I cared for, even if he'd had a part in my father finding me.

"*Fun*?" he snapped. "Young lady, you know what your mother and I are trying to accomplish for you. How could you be so stupid to risk that?"

It wasn't the first time I'd heard him say I was being stupid. Or that I *was* stupid. My father had a way with words.

"Are you OK?" Mom asked quietly. Once in a while, she exhibited a glimmer of caring about me and not just the family image.

Sometimes I wondered if she truly did love AJ and me and want the best for us but was also too far under my father's thumb. In reality, it didn't matter. She still allowed him to rule us with an iron fist.

"I'm fine. They took good care of us."

"I bet." The innuendo in my father's voice made my stomach turn.

"Better they leave us on the side of the road," Kenzie murmured, probably assuming that I'd be the only one to hear her.

She was wrong.

"I don't want to hear from you." My father spoke to her for the first time since we'd arrived. "You need to leave."

I furrowed my brows. "She can't. She doesn't have her car."

"It's fixed and sitting at her apartment. Donovan will drive her home."

I wasn't sure what to say at first given the amount of surprise filling me. My father had her car fixed. That was so weird. "You had it fixed?"

"Yes, well, once Donovan found it at the shop it had been towed to it seemed like the logical thing to do. Get it fixed and back here because you'd have to come for it eventually."

So he found it at the garage like I figured he would. As soon as it was somewhere it could be tracked, Donovan would've found it.

A quick glance over my shoulder found Donovan lurking near the door with only my suitcase next to him. He hadn't even brought Kenzie's from the car.

Her gaze locked with mine and I shrugged. There was no sense fighting it. "You better go," I told her.

She hurried over to me and pulled me tightly into her arms. "I'll call you."

"Neither of you is going off to war," my father bellowed. "Charlotte is going to spend some time with her family. That's all. You may go."

Kenzie released me but scowled at my father. I tried to send her a mental message to just go because her getting caught up in this would just make things worse.

Once the two of them were gone, I turned back to my parents.

"Listen, I'm twenty-one years old. I didn't do anything wrong. In fact, all I did was try to have a little bit of fun. Fun your gorilla watchman won't let me have."

"He's there to protect you."

"He's there to babysit me and you know it." I took a step closer. "I follow every stupid rule you've laid out because I wanted to avoid problems. This was one thing I wanted to do for me. I walk the straight and narrow because it's easier. I want to get through college. But I'm never going to be the person you want me to be. I'm not going into politics. Maybe have another kid and try again."

My mother scoffed. She'd made no secret about the fact that I had been a hard pregnancy and delivery. She never wanted to go through that again.

"Listen," I continued. Both of them were watching me so intently that it was hard to continue. In the past, the weight of their glares had kept me quiet. Small. That wasn't going to be me anymore. "I'll do my very best not to embarrass this family and I think I've done a good job so far. But I have to be able to be me."

"Charlotte." My father's teeth were clenched. He was not a man used to anyone standing up to him, let alone his children. AJ did now, but when he'd been younger, he'd just done what he'd wanted and hoped our father never found out.

"No. Don't 'Charlotte' me." Tears burned the backs of my eyes, but I wouldn't give him the satisfaction. "Kenzie and I were having fun. Nothing more. We weren't doing drugs... Hell, I didn't even have alcohol. We were doing what people our age do. A concert and a road trip. Neither of us expected to break down on the roadside."

"We were worried about the two of you," my mother told me.

"No. You weren't. You were worried I'd gone off the rails, but I didn't. I made some friends. Good people." I sighed because this conversation wouldn't matter to them in the morning. "Right now, I'm going to find a way home."

"You'll stay here," he commanded. "This is your home."

I shook my head. "I won't stay here. This has never been a home. It's a museum. I'm going home."

Though I had no idea how I'd get there. It took some time, but Kenzie got her car, then came right back to pick me up. It meant hiding out in my old room at the governor's mansion to avoid my parents and not ruin my fantastic exit, but I did it.

All I wanted was to get into bed and pretend that London hadn't hurt me because he didn't like my developing feelings. Or maybe it hadn't been him. He'd seemed so genuinely confused when I'd accused him. Either way, my heart was hurting.

19

LONDON

"What the fuck were you thinking?" I yelled into the kitchen. All eyes turned on me.

"Who are you talking to?" Grayson asked, but everyone had to know.

"Jamison. Why the fuck would you send Charlotte to the door?"

"Uh... because the guy asked for her."

"Jami..." Grayson shook his head.

"What? Someone comes to the door for someone, you send them to the door." He glanced around. "Right? That's a normal thing to do."

"It is," Lilah answered him.

"But we knew her father was looking for her.

How could you send her to that fucking door without..."

"Without what?" Lilah asked, like she already knew the answer.

I clenched my jaws and willed myself to calm the fuck down before I fucking outed myself. "Finding out who was asking."

"Why the fuck would I do that?" Jamison took a drink of the orange juice in front of him, as if he had no clue why I was upset.

"Jamison." Grayson turned to him. "We all knew that Charlotte's dad was looking for her."

"What?" Lilah asked, but he didn't turn to her. "Grayson." Still, he didn't respond. Right now, he was focused on Jamison.

"We did?" he asked, then realization dawned on him. "That's right. Sean told us."

"Yeah. He did." I ran a hand over my face as I sighed.

She was gone and for whatever fucked-up reason, she thought that I'd told the guy where she was.

First, why the fuck would I do that when... Well, never mind why I wouldn't do it, but I hadn't. None of us had. Second, I needed to decide what I was going to do about it, if anything.

I was leaning toward nothing. Our fling was going to be over in less than a week anyway. But there was no way I wanted it to end like that and the need to make sure they were all right took over.

"Who has Charlotte's number?" I asked the room.

"I would've thought you did, given the way you two have been," Lennox told me. Good assumption, but no. She'd never offered up her number and I'd never asked.

So I turned to the women.

"Not me," Becca said right away. "She has my number. Or Kenzie does."

"Me, either," Lilah agreed. "Charlotte wasn't using her phone. I didn't see her with it a single time. Now I figure it was because she didn't want her dad to track it. Which, by the way..." She raised an eyebrow at Grayson. "You all knew her father was looking for her? What's going on?"

"Yeah." Becca turned toward the room. "I thought we were all friends here. Why keep it from us?"

"Her father is the Governor of Michigan," Grayson explained. "He called Sean. No idea how he made the connection between finding Kenzie's car and us, but he did. We told Sean to not tell him she was with us."

"Well, if he's the governor, he probably has ways."

"Yeah."

We were all quiet until Lilah spoke a minute later. "She told me that she got a lot of pressure from her parents. It didn't seem like they hurt her, so that's good. Or at least not physically..."

I suddenly felt too big for my skin. Like it was stretched so tightly that I was going to Hulk out. The thought of Charlotte being taken back to those people turned my stomach. She wasn't afraid of her parents, but she wasn't happy under their thumbs.

Now I just wanted her back with us. Where I knew she was safe and happy.

And I wanted to know why the fuck she'd asked me how I could've done this. As if I'd sent her packing. Though I could see where she'd get the idea, I'd hoped she didn't think that kind of shit about me.

"Who has Kenzie's number?" I asked. She was the best way I could think of to get to Charlotte.

"I do." Becca pulled her phone from her pocket.

"I do too." Lilah didn't make a move to get her phone out, though.

But Becca was already on it. My phone dinged to

let me know that I had a text and when I checked it, she'd shared Kenzie's contact information.

I didn't use the number at first. It'd be like an hour and a half before they got to Lansing, assuming that was where she was headed. It would've been better to wait until she wasn't copped up in the car with that guy. I didn't even know if there was only one of them in the car. For all I knew, the phone could ring with a text and some goon would take it before either of the women saw that it was from me.

Fuck. What was the right thing to do?

I stomped through the kitchen, out the sliding door, then dropped into one of the chairs on the deck. The sun was so fucking bright, but I felt like I'd already lived the entire day.

Having Charlotte with me had been so fucking good that I hadn't appreciated it when she'd been here. I'd convinced myself that there were no feelings between us, nothing we wouldn't be able to get over with time. Even after she'd said she couldn't stop me from loving me even if I couldn't love her... That had been worse than being punched in the nuts.

It wasn't that I *couldn't* love her. Or someone. I didn't fucking *want* to. Let someone into your heart and you were open to that heart shattering. I'd done that once. I wasn't going to do it again.

None of that mattered here. I had to make sure Charlotte and Kenzie were OK. It took a while, but I worked up the nerve to make the phone call that I dreaded.

Kenzie had given me a dirty look before she'd left, which had me thinking that she thought it had been me too. It hadn't been. There was no fucking way any of us had given anyone information.

The phone rang twice before Kenzie answered.

"Hello?" She sighed into the phone.

"Where is she?" I asked. We both knew that was why I was calling. I mean, sure, I'd want to know that Kenzie was good too, but she wasn't the reason I'd called.

"At her parents'."

"Where are you?"

"Being driven home by a fucking yes-man," she said loudly.

A deep voice in the background asked, "Want to walk?"

"It'd be preferable."

"Kenzie," I snapped. "What the fuck is going on?"

She sighed again and returned her voice to

normal. No. Not normal. She lowered it as if trying to keep the man driving her from hearing her. "The guy at the door was Charlotte's dad's bodyguard. The guy he's had watching her since he won the election. Shit. Maybe before. I don't know."

"He had someone watching her?" Anger burned through me quick and hot with the force of mother nature. This guy was something else.

"Yup. That's why she never used her phone and worried about them finding her. Which they did. She worried that they'd make her go home. Which they did."

"Is she...?"

"She's fine. They don't hurt her. I think the big idiot driving me right now would if he needed to." There was a thump and a gasp out of Kenzie. "Asshole."

"Sorry. Thought I saw a deer." The masculine voice didn't sound sorry at all.

"Kenzie?" I pressed.

"Sorry. He hit the brakes hard, which slammed me forward."

"You're all right?" I asked.

"Peachy. Anyway. Charlotte is at her parents' house. Probably for a while." She lowered her voice more. "I plan to go get her once I'm back to my car."

"Good." I let the silence play in the air for a moment. "Do you have any idea why she thinks it was me who led her father to her?"

"I don't. But I'm going to find out. I'll let you know."

We ended the call there, which left me out on the deck alone with my thoughts. Kenzie had said she'd let me know and of course I'd noticed that she hadn't offered to give me Charlotte's phone number. Couldn't blame her, really.

Had I actually thought that I was going to let Charlotte go when we got back to Detroit and not think anything of it? If I had thought that, this proved how fucking wrong I was.

Within a few minutes of my phone call, I sent Kenzie a text asking for Charlotte's phone number. She replied saying to let her handle this.

It wasn't like I had a choice.

Everyone else had fun the rest of our days at the beach house. I'd say that I did too, but it was always with an asterisk. Fun-ish. But I worried about Charlotte and no matter how many times I asked Kenzie for her phone number, she wouldn't give it to me. All she'd tell me is that they were both fine.

That wasn't fucking good enough, but I didn't have a choice.

Even finally going to Becca and Lilah didn't help. Either they had the same information that I did or they weren't telling me.

By the time we were back on tour, I'd convinced myself that this was the reason I didn't get my fucking feelings involved.

"Who's coming with me tonight?" Jamison asked as we got ready for our show in Detroit.

The one Charlotte and Kenzie were supposed to be at, but when I asked Becca or Lilah if they were going to be there, neither knew for sure. They thought Kenzie would be and once they had confirmation, they were making plans to do something since we were in Detroit for two shows and staying at a hotel.

I'd stopped messaging Kenzie because it'd gotten weird. Not to mention she wasn't telling me anything anyway.

"Coming where?" Lennox asked.

"Wherever you can," Thatcher cried like a battle call.

I shook my head but couldn't help the jealousy that peeked in. Jealousy that they were so fucking carefree. Like I'd been before I'd turned into a brooding fucker.

"You guys are gross," Becca told them seriously.

"Nah, baby." Jamison slid his arm around her shoulders. "We're rock stars."

She made a gagging noise then stepped out from under his arm to continue steaming the clothes for tonight. Things got wrinkled in transit.

Before I could unleash the retort that was on the tip of my tongue, the door opened and Sean peeked his head through.

"You want to talk to me?" he asked, looking at me.

"Yeah."

I stopped what I was doing and headed for the door. We could talk in the hallway. It wasn't like this was personal, but I didn't need the guys hearing it.

"What's up?" he asked.

He was the only one with the information that I wanted, though I should've asked before this. "You didn't give Charlotte's dad any information on where she was, did you?"

He furrowed his brows. "Of course not. You guys said not to, so I didn't. Why?"

"No reason. I've just been trying to figure out how he found her."

Sean shrugged. "Who the fuck knows? He's the governor. I'd guess he has ways. Like knowing other governors who can have law enforcement look at traffic cameras or fucking ask around."

"True." I wet my lips quickly.

"Why are you asking now?"

I took a deep breath. "Before she left, she said that she couldn't believe I could do something like that, tell her dad where to find her, but I didn't do shit."

"Then she's a fucking idiot."

I scowled. "Come on, man."

He held up a hand. "Sorry."

After she left, I stopped trying to pretend that she wasn't important to me whenever someone was around or brought her up.

I wasn't using the L word or any bullshit like that, but I knew that my schedule for tomorrow before the show was going to include me trying to find her in Ann Arbor. Hopefully, with Kenzie's help. Even if she'd been less-than-helpful to me.

"Thanks," I told him then went back to the dressing room where Becca and Lilah were happily giggling. "What's going on with them?" I asked Grayson, who was the closest.

He didn't have a chance to answer before Lilah did. "Kenzie's coming to the show, so we're going to hang out tonight."

My heart thudded against my chest and my stomach tightened. If she was coming, then maybe—

"She didn't say if Charlotte was coming with her or not," Becca offered. "We asked, but she didn't know one way or another."

Of course she didn't. Because Kenzie wasn't being helpful. To us. I was sure she was helping Charlotte and that was what mattered.

20

CHARLOTTE

I'd spent the week in negotiations. Negotiations with my parents and AJ, who decided to stay at my apartment rather than with my parents. It'd been a busy week, but a good one. I hadn't spent that much time with my brother in too long. Plus, he was there to help me manage my parents.

I didn't have to reason with them. I could've told them to fuck off and gone out on my own, but that would've caused more problems than it solved. I'd sacrificed so much to get through college and I wasn't going to quit with only one year left. I could do one mor year of this but something that being with Forever 18 taught me about myself was that I needed things to change at least a little.

My father's family may have been out of the mob business, but the mental game of it remained.

When it came down to it, my parents were going to let me live my life without a babysitter. Poor Donovan would be doing lord-knew-what for my father.

Now my father tried to play it off as if it were for my own good. I was a woman on a college campus whose father was going to run for president. He said that made me vulnerable. I told him that I could handle myself.

Could I? I thought so, but we were about to find out.

"I can't believe you don't have that big dude following you around anymore," Kenzie told me as we got ready for the concert in Detroit. I hadn't decided to go until she was getting ready. Since we already had tickets and I liked Forever 18, why the hell not?

That was my new life motto: Why the hell not?

"I know," I told her. "It'll take some time to get used to not looking over my shoulder to see if he was getting too close."

"Is my little girl going to get wasted for the first time tonight?"

I giggled at the idea that held no appeal for me. "Absolutely not."

"Seriously?"

I shook my head. "I'll have a drink like I always do, but the idea of not being in control of myself freaks me out. I don't think I ever want to get drunk."

She nodded knowingly. "I get it. That's why I don't drink to excess. I have before, but the next day... It's not worth it."

"You know." I stopped putting my makeup on. "I think somewhere deep down in my mother, she went along with all this because she actually cares about us. Not enough to protect us from an overbearing father, but something."

She put her arms around me. "I think they both care." When she pulled back, she added, "In their own fucked-up way."

The two of us laughed because there was no other way to describe my parents' parenting skills.

"So what'd they agree to?" she asked.

"I won't have a shadow anymore," I told her which was the most surprising part.

"Are you serious?"

I nodded. "I made it clear that I'm not going into politics and am opening a shelter after graduation."

"One that never turns animals away, right?"

"Yes." It was a lofty dream but I was determined.

My father even said he wouldn't try to hold up my trust fund as long as I agreed to remember what family I came from and do my best not to cause any scandals.

That had been easy to agree to. Causing a scene wasn't something I wanted to do anyway. Oh, and I had to participate in the events that my schedule allowed. He was going to run for president, even if he hadn't announced yet. Right now, it was all rumor on the news. That meant there were times he would need to put out his happy family. Happy family. Yeah. OK.

With everything settled, I was finally my own adult.

The first thing on my agenda was to talk to London. I'd accused him of conspiring with my father, which he'd denied immediately and he deserved an apology. It might not change anything else, but I wouldn't be OK with myself until I did it.

Kenzie and I were climbing into my car to head to Detroit. It was early, but we were going to see the girls and it was a bit of a drive.

"Why wouldn't you let me tell Becca and Lilah that you were coming with me?" she asked halfway through the tip. "I told her that I didn't know one way or another."

"Honestly?" I asked. She nodded. "I was worried I'd back out then they'd be disappointed."

"Uh-huh." She didn't believe me.

"I was also worried that London would find out and keep me from coming." That was harder to admit than I thought it would be. Especially to Kenzie.

"Why would he do that?"

I shrugged. "Fears aren't fears because there's logic behind them."

"Lilah says he's asked for your phone number. They couldn't give it to them because they don't have it."

Oh. Right. "Shoot. I forgot. I'll give it to them today."

"You're going to see him, right?"

"It's his show. Of course I'm going to see him."

She cocked her head to the side, so I didn't bother glancing over. "You know that's not what I mean."

"I know." I sighed. "Yes. If he'll see me, I'd like to talk to him. Apologize because he deserves it."

She made a noise in her throat, which told me how much she disagreed with that statement, but she didn't hear the way I'd spoken to him. He deserved an apology because he hadn't done anything. London had been upfront about what he'd been willing to give me and what he hadn't been. I couldn't be mad at him for sticking to that.

We changed the subject back to our normal chatter, which now included a lot of talk about my plans for after school. It was new and exciting. I'd told her to shut me up when it became too much, but she was almost as excited as I was.

The closer we got to the venue, the more nervous I became.

Knowing London, he wouldn't be an asshole to me or turn me away. Though that might've been preferable.

I pulled into the parking lot slow and the minute I did, my heart rate picked up and my palms started sweating.

"Calm down," Kenzie told me. "It'll be fine. London's not going to make a scene or anything."

"I know. I'm fine." Though I was anything but.

I'd missed talking to him so much over the last week. The other stuff too, but just talking to him was what I missed most.

We were barely out of the car when there was a squeal. Lilah and Becca were by the door. We'd parked as far back as we could near the buses and the entrance we knew the band would be using.

Kenzie and I hurried over to them and the four of us exchanged hugs like it'd been a year since we last saw them.

"I'm so glad you decided to come," Lilah said once she'd let me go. "We've missed you."

"I wasn't going to," I told her. "But then she was getting dressed and I had to." I had been teetering back and forth even though I'd told Kenzie I was going. I'd figured that I could always backout if I decided to.

"Of course you did!" Becca squealed a little again. "Do you two still have your All-Access passes?"

I shook my head because I hadn't thought those would be good anymore and because I wasn't sure they'd want us to use them. Honestly, I thought I'd messed it all up for the both of us.

"No problem," Lilah assured us. "We'll have Sean get you new ones. That way, you can come and go as you please for the weekend. Are you two staying at the same hotel?"

"I don't think we're staying." I glanced at Kenzie, who had a grin on her face. "Or maybe we are."

"Yeah. I made a reservation."

"Kenzie!" I sighed. "I didn't bring any other clothes. I thought we were going home then driving in tomorrow."

She shrugged. "You have your bag in the car."

"Those are backup clothes. In case I spill or something. I didn't bring any makeup."

"You don't need any," Lilah assured me, "but you can use mine. Or Becca's. She has the same coloring as you."

I sighed again. There wasn't anything I could do about it and if there was something I needed, I could run to a store. "I guess I can buy anything else I need."

Kenzie wrapped an arm around my shoulders and bumped my hip with hers. "That's the spirit."

The four of us were catching up on what had happened, though I left out the stuff with my parents. We could talk about that when we were more comfortable. It was going to take a lot of explaining.

"Hey, guys," Lilah called out over my head, which caused both Kenzie and me to turn.

Grayson and London were walking across the parking lot, each with a to-go coffee cup in his hand, laughing at whatever.

London looked so good. Tall. His dark hair the right kind of messy.

I'd missed him and his jeans. Not to mention the black T-shirt with the V-neck and the way they fit his body.

That was only what I could see from the short distance. His smile faltered when he saw me, but he recovered.

Once the greetings were done, Lilah suggested the four of us get something to eat. It was past lunchtime and she was starving.

"Sure," I agreed. "But I was hoping I could talk to London first." I finally turned to him to find him gazing down at me.

He took a second but then said, "Yeah. That's fine."

The two of us walked away, me following him.

"Don't take up all of her time!" Becca yelled.

London raised a middle finger over his shoulder without looking back, which got him laughter from the entire group we'd left behind.

He took us around the corner, where I saw a couple of benches. When he took a seat, I did the same. My nerves were on edge. Butterflies were flapping away in my chest and I was twisting my fingers around each other the way I did when I was nervous.

London laid a hand over mine to get me to stop.

"What's up?" he asked, watching me with those dark eyes. Dark eyes that were utterly unreadable.

"I want to apologize to you."

His brows furrowed. "For?"

I wet my suddenly dry lips with my tongue that felt like the Sahara. This was harder than even I'd imagined.

"Before I left... I basically accused you of telling my father where we were to get rid of me." His jaw clenched. "That wasn't fair. I'm sorry."

He took a slow drink of his coffee before acknowledging my words then set it on the ground near him. Those moments were sheer torture. "Apology accepted. Did you find out how he found you?"

I shook my head. "Not exactly, but I asked who told him and he said Donovan did. Since Donovan was the one who said it was you, or the band anyway, I assume he was just making trouble. They tracked her car to the repair shop."

"I hate that guy. Never met him but hate him anyway."

I let out a quiet laugh. "Yeah. Join the club. But I'm no longer saddled with him, so it doesn't matter."

"No?"

I shook my head again. "No. My parents and I have come to an understanding, so I'm not mostly out from beneath their thumbs."

"Mostly?"

I took a deep breath. "Well, yeah. They are still paying for school and my father has promised not to hold up my trust fund when I graduate."

He raised his eyebrows. "In exchange for what?"

"I have to make some appearances when my schedule allows. Can't have the future President of the United States have an estranged child, now can we?"

"He's really running for president?"

I nodded but said, "I'm not voting for him." London smiled, but I hated the feeling that our conversation was coming to an end. Wetting my lips again had no effect on the dry feeling. "So anyway, I wanted to apologize and you accepted. I'm hoping we can be friends."

"Friends?"

I nodded. "Yeah. That's what I want anyway. You were completely upfront about everything, so there's no reason for us to not be friends." I swallowed hard. "Right?"

"Do you remember what you said the night before you left?"

Of course I did. That was what had me nervous about this. "It won't be a problem."

"But it *is* a problem."

I sighed. "London, what I said is true. You can lock everyone out forever, but you can't control how they feel about you." I shrugged. "I'm not sorry I said it, but you don't have to worry about it."

"It got me thinking," he continued, as if he hadn't heard what I'd just said. "That's why I can't be friends with you."

The next words out of my mouth felt like sandpaper. "I understand."

When I made a move to get up off the bench, his hand snaked out and rested on the back of my neck. Firmly, but not tightly. My eyes grew wide as London moved in closer. His lips were almost to mine when he said, "I can't be friends with you because I think I fell in love with you this week while you were gone."

Shock. That was the only way to describe hearing him say that and when his lips crashed into mine. I reached up to take his head in my hands, cupping his jaw as it worked. He slipped his arms around me and pulled me onto his lap.

I didn't care that we were in public or that I was wearing a skirt and could feel his hardness under the thin material of my panties.

All I cared was that London was kissing me and couldn't be my friend. Everything else fell away. London slid his hands down to my waist then pressed me against him. He swallowed my groan then deepened the kiss.

"We need to find somewhere more private," he said when he pulled back. At first, I didn't get what he meant, but he pushed me firmly into his erection again.

I leaned in to kiss him again, but it was hard to keep the smile off my face. Which made it hard to kiss him properly.

"Do you think I'm joking?" he asked once we broke the kiss again.

"No." I moved to climb off his lap, but his firm hands held me in place.

He brushed his fingers across my cheek and into my hair. "I love you, Charlotte. It's very hard for me to admit that. But I'm going to need you to promise that nothing's going to happen to you."

My heart swelled and hurt for him at the same time. "I promise, London. Nothing's going to happen to me." Realistically, we both knew there was no guarantee of that, but if he needed me to promise it every single day, I would. "I love you, too."

"All right." He stood, holding on to me for a

moment before letting me slide down his body to get my feet on the ground. "I know Lilah and Becca want to go eat, but are you hungry?"

"I can wait."

"Good."

He led me back around to where we'd left everyone else. They were still there talking and laughing. It might've felt like London and I had been gone forever, given everything that had passed between us, but it'd only been a few minutes.

This time, though, he had my hand wrapped in his.

When we got up there, I noticed Grayson raise an eyebrow at London, who shrugged. "I can't be friends with her." He'd answered the unasked question.

"I didn't think you could be," Grayson said back, but the girls seemed all confused until they noticed him holding my hand. Luckily, none of them said anything about it.

"So... lunch?" Lilah asked the group.

"Yeah," London answered. "You go ahead. Charlotte and I need about twenty minutes."

I snorted but held in a laugh. So London leaned over and whispered, "I'll be quick."

"We'll figure out where we're eating and text

you." She was also trying not to laugh. "Oh, Charlotte, I need your phone number."

"Yeah. Me too." London nudged my arm.

That was right. I hadn't given any of them my number because I hadn't been using my phone last week. "Everyone can have it today."

"I'll give it to Lilah and Becca." Kenzie gave me a gentle shove. "We'll meet you there."

As Grayson pulled me away, Kenzie yelled, "Don't be *impolite* to my friend."

Once again, London lifted his middle finger over his shoulder without looking back.

"You like it when I'm impolite," he explained after opening the door on the bus.

"Yes. Yes I do."

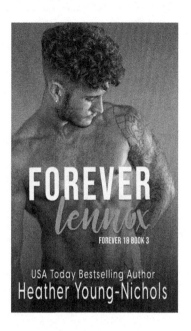

FOREVER Lennox

Forever 18 Book 3

He's wanted her longer than he wants to admit but she's his band mate's sister. Totally off limits. Now that she's with them on tour... he won't be able to keep away from her.

Preorder Forever Lennox today!

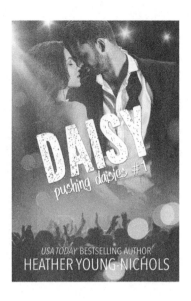

He insists she's too young for him but she's determined to prove him wrong.

DAISY

Pushing Daisies 1

Daisy owns the stage every night. I can't help being pulled into her world with the crowd as she sings and captivates all of us. And she's so damn beautiful but more than that... she's a good person. Daisy's also too young for me.

Which is why, when her manager tells me that

they've been getting disturbing messages involving Daisy, I know that I'll do everything in my power to protect her.

Grab Daisy today!

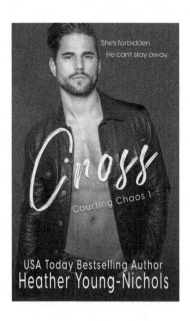

A sexy drummer and a rock god's daughter... what could possibly go wrong?

CROSS

Courting Chaos 1

What bigger mistake could I make than to call the sexy, sassy daughter of the man could make or break us a groupie?

Oh. I could also try to kick her out of the arena.

Better yet, I could not be able to get her out of my mind. Indie is off limits.

I don't seem to care.

Hooking up with her could definitely ruin our big break and we already have our bassist determined to do that.

Still I can't stay away.

Grab Cross today!

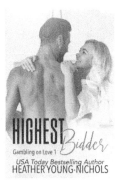  

Are you ready to take a gamble?

Meet three friends who are and fall in love right along with them!

Check out the Gambling on Love Series today!

 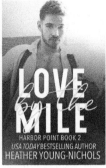 

Take a trip to Harbor Point!

Harbor Point: a tourist trap with hot men, hot pizza, and the women who will change everything!

Check out the Harbor Point Series today!

Prepare for the fallout!

Returning home leads to discovering a lie that could ruing everything.

Check out The Fallout Series today!

To stay up to date on all the things, get exclusive access to ARCs and give-aways, and be a member of a fun, positive, drama-free space, join Sweet and Sexy with a Side of Snark.

About the Author

Heather Young-Nichols is a USA Today Bestselling author of contemporary and paranormal romance. A native of the great and often very cold state of Michigan, she is better known at home and to her friends as the Snarker-in-Chief. A job she excels at beyond anything she could have imagined. She loves many things, but especially cold coffee, hot books, and baseball. But not necessarily in that order.

Find Heather on Social Media or by visiting her website.

heatheryoungnichols.com

facebook.com/heatheryoungnicholsauthor

instagram.com/heatheryoungnichols

amazon.com/Heather-Young-Nichols/e/B00KKTM54A

bookbub.com/authors/heather-young-nichols

tiktok.com/@heatheryoungnichols

Made in the USA
Coppell, TX
25 August 2022

82061193R00166